THE BENNING LEGACY: Three sisters find true love uncovers the secrets of the past... and forges bright new tomorrows!

Have I Ever Wanted A Man More?

The question was deadly, reminding Sierra of her amnesia. Reluctantly she broke from Clint's embrace, instantly missing the warmth and power of his touch.

"I'm sorry," he said. "I shouldn't have touched you, but I couldn't resist."

"I know." Sierra knew he was honorable, but the attraction between them was powerful. She shuddered as the enormity of her situation hit her. Was she falling in love with Clint? What if a husband or lover should suddenly come to light…?

"Good night," she whispered huskily before going in.

Clint stayed outside, looking over his spread. He wanted Sierra to get well; he could never wish for anything else.

But when she did, everything would change....

Dear Reader,

August predictably brings long steamy days…and hot sensuous nights. And this month Silhouette Desire spotlights the kind of pure passion that can erupt only in that sizzling summer climate.

Get ready to fall head over heels for August's MAN OF THE MONTH, a sexy rancher who opens his home (and his heart?) to a lost beauty desperately hoping to recover her memory in *A Montana Man* by Jackie Merritt. Bestselling author Cait London continues her hugely popular miniseries THE TALLCHIEFS with *Rafe Palladin: Man of Secrets.* Rafe is an irresistible takeover tycoon with a plan to *acquire* a Tallchief lady. Barbara McMahon brings readers the second story in her IDENTICAL TWINS! duo—in *The Older Man* an exuberant young woman is swept up by her love and desire for a tremendously gorgeous, *much* older man.

Plus, talented Susan Crosby unfolds a story of seduction, revenge and scandal in the continuation of THE LONE WOLVES with *His Seductive Revenge.* And TEXAS BRIDES are back with *The Restless Virgin* by Peggy Moreland, the story of an innocent Western lady tired of waiting around for marriage—so she lassos herself one unsuspecting cowboy! And you've never seen a hero like *The Consummate Cowboy,* by Sara Orwig. He's all man, all-around ornery and all-out tempted…by his ex-wife's sister!

I know you'll enjoy reading all six of this sultry month's brand-new Silhouette Desire novels by some of the most beloved and sexy authors of romance.

Regards,

Melissa Senate

Melissa Senate
Senior Editor
Silhouette Books

Please address questions and book requests to:
Silhouette Reader Service
U.S.: 3010 Walden Ave., P.O. Box 1325, Buffalo, NY 14269
Canadian: P.O. Box 609, Fort Erie, Ont. L2A 5X3

JACKIE MERRITT
A MONTANA MAN

SILHOUETTE *Desire*®

Published by Silhouette Books

America's Publisher of Contemporary Romance

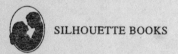 SILHOUETTE BOOKS

ISBN 0-373-76159-7

A MONTANA MAN

Printed in U.S.A.

JACKIE MERRITT

and her husband live in the Southwest. An accountant for many years, Jackie has happily traded numbers for words. Next to family, books are her greatest joy. She started writing in 1987, and her efforts paid off in 1988 with the publication of her first novel. When she's not writing or enjoying a good book, Jackie dabbles in watercolor painting, and she likes playing the piano in her spare time.

One

Clint Barrow urged the horse he was riding up a rocky knoll. It was early morning. There was enough light to see by even though the sun hadn't yet risen above the mountain tops, and wispy patches of ground fog drifted within dips of the mountainous country all around him. At the top of the knoll he pulled on the reins and stopped his horse. This was a favorite spot in which to view his ranch, and below his vantage point Barrow land spread almost as far as Clint could see. The buildings appeared as miniatures, and cattle and horses looked toy-like. Clint breathed a sigh of contentment.

He was a big man, tall and rangy, with dark hair and vivid blue eyes. His contentment was genuine. The shock of his one major tragedy in life, the death of his wife, had softened with time. He had a seventeen-year-old son,

Tommy, on which to expend his love, and this ranch. He was the first person in the area to help out a friend or a neighbor in trouble, and, all in all, life was good. He felt strongly that no man should ask for more.

As the sun suddenly showed its face on the eastern horizon, Clint turned his horse's head and rode back down the knoll toward the ranch compound. Tommy would be leaving for school shortly, and Clint liked to be there every morning to say a few words to his son before he left. Today it seemed even more important; today was the start of Tommy's final exams. High school graduation was just around the corner. Unlike too many of the fathers and sons that Clint knew, he and Tommy were close, and Clint knew that he would do almost anything to protect their special relationship.

He arrived at the compound just as Tommy was coming out of the house and heading for his red pickup truck.

"Morning, Dad," Tommy called.

"Morning, Tom." Clint dismounted and let his horse go. He wouldn't go far, Clint knew, and would, in fact, come back to him with a whistle.

"Looks like we're in for a nice day," Tommy said as he opened the door of his truck.

"Sure does." Clint glanced at his watch. "You're running a little late."

"I know. Better get going. I gotta pick up Eric."

"Are you sure you have time for that?"

"I told him I'd pick him up this morning, Dad." Tommy grinned and swung himself up into the truck. "Remember, Barrows don't go back on their word."

Clint had to smile. He had instilled in his son the value of a man keeping his word. It was his own credo and he believed that honor was the primary difference between men of principle and those hapless individuals who drifted through life without hope, ambition or inspiration.

"Well, drive safely," he told his son. "See you this evening."

Tommy started the motor and rolled down the window. "See ya, Dad."

Clint stood in the yard and watched the red pickup travel the driveway, his pride swelling in his chest. There were moments like this when he became very emotional about his son. Tommy would soon graduate from high school, he was no longer Clint's "little boy." He was teetering between manhood and childhood, and would go away to college in the fall. Clint could only hope that Tommy would want to return to the ranch after he completed his education.

When Clint could no longer see the red pickup, he whistled for his horse. It trotted over and Clint climbed into the saddle. It was time for his own day to begin.

Five days earlier.

Sierra's new minivan was loaded to the roof with clothes, personal mementos and all of her painting supplies—rolled canvases, stretcher boards, tubes of oil paints, boxes of brushes and palette knives, easels, as well as several gallon cans of turpentine, which she used to clean her equipment.

She had packed carefully, and everything was snugly fitted together in the vehicle. The only unfilled space was the very front of the van, and even then her purse, maps and a notebook and pen lay on the passenger seat, where she could easily reach them from the driver's seat. Her bank account had been converted to five hundred dollars in cash and the rest in traveler's checks. She carried no credit cards, and her wallet contained only her driver's license and the cash.

She was dressed for comfort in loose-fitting denim pants and a sweatshirt. Her long dark hair had been confined into one braid, and her face was devoid of makeup. Her skin was deep toned, appearing suntanned year-round; she had never needed cosmetics to enhance her coloring. She was thirty-three years old and looked five years younger.

Her figure was exceptionally good, as firm as it had been during her college years when she had first met Mike. They had dated for a while, she had wondered how deep her feelings really were for Mike Findley, then graduation had separated them. She'd known he was going on to law school, and she had found a job in an art gallery and polished her talent with oil paints and private lessons. Eventually she had moved to San Francisco, recalling only absentmindedly that Mike's family lived there. She'd thought of him occasionally, but never dreamed they would ever see each other again.

It had happened. She'd been at a party, and had hardly believed her own eyes when Mike walked up to her. "Sierra? Sierra Benning? Is it really you?" he'd said with the grin she had found so irresistible in college.

This time love had bloomed at once, and they had married after three months of romance and laughter, of dining and dancing, of Mike introducing her to his friends and his family, of her being showered with gifts and flowers and sweet little love notes. Their wedding had been...

"No," she said out loud, denying herself both the pain and the luxury of reliving that special day. The memories would always be there, but she needn't deliberately drag them out and cause herself more heartache.

She didn't understand Mike's infidelity and knew she never would. While he had been showing her how much he loved her in dozens of ways, he had been meeting other women in hotel rooms. She had slept very little last night, wondering what might be ahead of her, thinking of the past and the disintegration of her marriage, knowing she was doing the right thing by breaking all ties but still not completely at ease with her plans.

The uneasiness would pass, she told herself. It had been a long time since she had taken a car trip by herself; con-

cern was only natural, especially since she had no destination in mind.

It was time to leave. There was sunshine this morning,
though the temperature was almost cool because of a breeze
off the Bay. Sierra stood next to her van and looked at the
glistening white mansion that had been her home for so
long. During that time span she had gone from delirious
happiness to acute misery.

It was over—all of it. Over with and behind her. She
could look at her marriage as years of wasted time, or she
could view her marriage and divorce as a lesson in life's
harsher realities. It was both, actually, and maybe that was
good. Certainly she would have to know a man inside and
out before she risked her heart again.

Thinking of the irony of it all delayed her departure for
another few minutes. Last week she had been a wealthy
woman; today everything she owned fit into one relatively
small space—the minivan. Ironic or not, she did not regret
negating the divorce settlement. Her own attorney had refused to help her do something so "utterly ridiculous"—
his exact words—so she had called Mike's. He had been
most helpful. In fact, he'd drawn up the papers with a haste
that had struck Sierra as funny, as though he, like most of
her friends, had been wondering if she'd lost her mind, and
wanted to get her signature on the documents before she
came to her senses.

God, why was she thinking of that now? Clearing her
mind with a slight shake of her head, Sierra slid behind the
wheel of the van and turned the ignition key. She drove
away from the Findley mansion without looking back. Her
uppermost thought was that she was going to try very hard
not to look back ever again. From this moment forward,
she would concentrate on the future. She had one—somewhere. All she had to do was find it.

It seemed that the farther Sierra got from San Francisco,
the braver she became about traveling alone. The traveling

itself was exciting, and she wanted to just go on and on. She felt absolutely wonderful and completely freed of the Findleys' influence.

Four days later she found herself in western Montana. She stayed in a motel in a very small settlement in the mountains that night, and went to the only café for dinner. There were a few other people in the place, and the waitress had greeted her with a friendly smile.

"Would you like to order now, or are you waiting for someone to join you?" the woman asked.

Sierra smiled. "If I waited for someone to join me, I'd starve to death."

"You're traveling alone?"

"That I am. I'll have the pot roast and hot tea."

"Good choice. Pot roast is the cook's best dish." The waitress smiled conspiratorially and dropped her voice. "Probably 'cause it's easy to fix."

Sierra laughed and laid down her menu. While the waitress went to turn in the order and get the tea, Sierra looked around. It was a quaint little café, with wood-paneled walls and linoleum flooring. The red checked tablecloths matched the curtains, and a cowbell over the door announced everyone leaving or arriving.

The waitress delivered hot water and a teabag. "Where're you heading, if you don't mind my asking?"

"Nowhere in particular." Sierra smiled. "Just wandering around. This area is beautiful, and I'd like to see more of it. I grew up in northern Idaho, but if you can believe it, I've never been in Montana before."

"Well, you be careful where you wander in these parts. This is a wilderness area, and it can be mighty dangerous."

"Oh, I plan to stay on the main roads. I mean, I have no intention of hiking around by myself. Tell me this. Are there people living in these mountains?"

"Oh, sure, but they're few and far between. Some real

nice ranches in the back country.''

"Where do the children attend school?''

"In Hillman. It's a little town about twenty miles from here.''

Sierra smiled. "Well, if the roads are safe for school buses, they certainly should be safe for my van.''

"The main roads are fine, miss, but the back roads can be treacherous. I advise strangers to stick to the highway. The weather's a bit deceiving, you know. Spring has sprung and the highway is clear at this elevation, but you could run into some snow and ice at higher altitudes.'' The woman looked concerned. "Don't see many women traveling alone up here. Just be careful.'' She walked off to help another customer.

Sierra pondered the warning. Was she being rash? Reckless? But she felt so…adventurous. Never in her life had she taken such an extended road trip, and she had already seen so many places and sights she hadn't known existed. She couldn't spend all her money touring the country, of course, but a day or so in this high country was really too appealing to resist.

She made up her mind. She would be careful—it was only sensible—but she *was* going to do some exploring. After all, she might never pass this way again.

Wednesday, May 21

Sierra dug through her bags and boxes for a warm jacket. The predawn air was cold enough to make her shiver, and the windows of her van were completely frosted over.

She had retired early last night, slept well and was anxious to be on her way, but she forced herself into the café for some breakfast as she had no idea when she would run across another place in which to eat. With that in mind, in addition to a large breakfast, she ordered some sandwiches

to go. An older man was waiting tables this morning, and
while he was as friendly as last night's waitress had been,
he was too busy for lengthy conversations with any one
customer.

Sierra went to the counter to pay her check and noticed
a rack of window scrapers for sale. It was one item she
didn't have with her, and she'd been wondering how she
was going to clear the van's windows of such heavy frost.

She walked out of the café with her bag of sandwiches
and a sturdy plastic scraper, pleased that she'd thought to
buy something for lunch and relieved about the frost problem.

She started the van's engine and turned on the defroster,
then got to work with the scraper. It took a full ten minutes
to clear the windows, but finally she was behind the wheel
and on the road again. About two miles from the small
settlement, the road became ascending. While the forest
was mostly heavy on each side, there were some open
spaces that permitted Sierra a view of dawn's first light.

It was going to be a fabulous day, she thought with a
zing of exhilaration, and although the ascending road was
narrow and quite curvy, there was very little traffic and she
felt completely in control. Turning on the radio, she found
a station playing country music, and sang along with Garth
Brooks. It had been so long since she'd felt like this, un-
burdened and lighthearted, and she cherished the sensation.
Life *could* be good, she thought with a contented sigh.
Leaving San Francisco had been the wisest decision she
had ever made.

The road twisted and wound its way upward, full dawn
broke and occasionally the trees parted to give Sierra a
breathtaking view of the mountains. It was still very early,
and only in those clearings did she actually see the sun.

The miles clicked by, and after a while Sierra noticed a
sign indicating another road up ahead. When she got to it

there was a second sign with an arrow pointing right and an inscription: Cougar Mountain.

She pulled onto the shoulder and consulted her map. But she couldn't locate that road on it, although she could pretty much tell where she was on the highway. A daring little smile toyed with her lips. Was she adventurous enough to leave the highway and drive a road that wasn't on the map? It looked safe enough from where she was parked. It was narrow, to be sure, but it was paved and appeared no more dangerous than the highway she was on.

She would do it! Why not? she thought as she got the van moving and made the turn. She could always turn around and head back to the highway if the road proved to be treacherous. Other than a little time, what did she have to lose?

She had just gone over the first hill when she spotted a river running parallel to the road. Moving swiftly in its rocky bed, it was just about the prettiest river Sierra had ever seen. She was driving slowly enough to take her eyes off the road and keep track of the river's path, and it was a delight to watch.

It was on her right, and after a few miles it seemed to be dropping below the road's level, while the road itself climbed higher. Another few miles and it was out of sight, probably at the bottom of a chasm that appeared to be getting deeper.

There was only a bit of shoulder between the road and the drop-off, and Sierra found herself hugging the center line. That deep chasm so close to the roadway made her a little nervous, and she wondered if she shouldn't turn around and go back to the highway.

Only there was no place to turn around. On the left side of the road was a rocky cliff, on the right was that deep ravine, and the road itself was too narrow for a U-turn. She had no choice but to keep going until she came to a wide spot. There must be one somewhere up ahead, she told herself. Just take it easy, drive cautiously and you'll come to it. The radio was a distraction now, and she switched it off.

The road kept climbing. Sierra spotted patches of old snow on the rocky bluff on her left, and her nervousness became more pronounced. She'd told the waitress last night that she was going to stick to the main highways, and she knew now that she should have done exactly that.

There was a blind curve just ahead, and she bit down on her bottom lip because it looked as though the road was heading directly for the ravine. It wouldn't, of course; it would wind around that outcropping of rock, and who knew? Maybe just beyond it would be a place wide enough for her to get turned around.

Suddenly a red pickup truck came bulleting around that curve, *on her side of the road!* Sierra slammed on the brakes and the van went into a skid. The truck also began skidding, and fishtailing, and its back end slapped against the van with tremendous force. Sierra screamed as the van nosed into the ravine. She saw the river at the bottom, and the boulders and rocks rushing up to meet her. The van began somersaulting, and Sierra's last coherent act was to unfasten her seat belt.

Two young men jumped out of the pickup and ran to the edge of the ravine. Frozen with dread, they stood there and watched the van tumbling down the rocky slope end over end, almost in slow motion, each bounce twisting the van's metal body into a different configuration.

"Tommy…Tommy…what should we do?" Eric Schulze cried.

They watched in horror as the driver's door flew open and a woman was thrown out onto the rocks. The next instant the van hit bottom, mere inches from the wildly rushing river.

"We have to go down there and see if she's okay."

Tommy Barrow was already on his way. Eric followed. It was tough going. One misstep and they could end up like that van—or worse, in the river.

Breathing hard, they finally reached Sierra. She was lying facedown and not moving. "I think she's dead," Eric said, his voice cracking.

Tommy knelt down and felt for a pulse. "She's alive. Eric, go check the van and make sure she was the only one in it, then go back to the truck, get to the nearest phone and call for help. I'll stay here."

"But…"

Tommy raised tear-filled eyes to his friend. "If she dies, it's my fault. I was driving too fast. I took that curve too wide. Go, Eric. Do it now. I can't leave her alone."

Eric started backing away. "Her van is smashed all to hell. Tommy! It's on fire!"

"What?" He stood up to see. "Oh, God, what if it explodes?" He ran as hard as he could over the rocks to peer inside the van. Hurrying back, he said with some relief, "There's no one else. Eric, we have to move this lady."

"You aren't supposed to move anyone hurt in an accident. What if her back is broken, or something?"

"She has no chance at all if we *don't* move her and that van explodes. Come on, help me turn her over."

The boys got down on their knees and very gently turned Sierra over onto her back. "You take her feet," Tommy said, moving into position to lift her by her shoulders. He glanced at the van. "The fire's getting worse. Everything inside is blazing. Hurry, Eric, hurry!"

"Where are we taking her?" Eric anxiously asked. "The canyon's so steep. We can't carry her clear up to the road."

Tommy took a quick look around. "Over there, behind that big boulder. Come on, let's get moving."

They had just lowered Sierra to the ground behind the boulder when the van exploded. The boys gaped at the sight.

"Holy cow," Tommy whispered. "She would have been killed for sure." He tore his eyes from the conflagration to look at Eric. "Get going and make that call. She's unconscious and could be hurt bad."

They both jumped a foot when a second explosion shook the canyon. This one was much worse than the first, and what was left of the van and its contents either fluttered to the rocks in minute pieces or landed in the river.

"It's gone," Eric said, as though he couldn't believe his own eyes. "Totally gone."

Two

John Mann of the Montana Highway Patrol introduced himself to Clint and Tommy Barrow, who rose from their chairs and shook hands with the officer. They were all tall men, and their eyes were almost on the same level. Officer Mann probably outweighed the Barrows, as Clint and his son were both lean and lanky, very much alike in appearance with dark hair and blue eyes.

Mann moved a chair from another part of the waiting room to sit closer to the Barrows. They were in the intensive care unit of Missoula General Hospital, where Sierra had been brought by a flight-for-life helicopter.

Officer Mann, big and burly as he was, spoke in a surprisingly soft voice. "Any news on the woman's condition?" he asked.

"Nothing conclusive. We've talked to a couple of doctors and several nurses. They're running tests," Clint said in a voice choppy from strain. As concerned as he was about the woman in room 217, he was more worried about his son. Tommy's face was pasty and gray. It could have been Tommy who had crashed at the bottom of that ravine, and Clint couldn't get that image out of his mind. The thought of losing his son in a car accident had Clint half sick to his stomach.

"Then she's regained consciousness?" John asked, looking from father to son.

"If she has, we haven't been told about it." Clint noticed John's close scrutiny of Tommy, and shifted in his chair so his shoulder touched his son's.

Officer Mann registered the protective gesture and cleared his throat. "It was a serious accident and will have to be investigated."

"Yes, I know," Clint said. The stern lines of his handsome face became even more rigid. If Tommy hadn't gone out of his way to pick up Eric for school, would there have been an accident? Clint knew that same question was haunting Tommy. The boys were the best of friends. Clint remembered his and Tommy's conversation before the boy had driven off in his red pickup that morning.

"You're running late, Tom."

"I told Eric I'd pick him up. Remember, Dad, Barrows don't go back on their word."

"Figured you did," Mann said quietly. "Well, let's get started." He produced a small note pad and a pen from an inside pocket of his jacket and flipped it open to a specific page. "Thomas Lee Barrow and Eric Roger Schulze," he read and glanced up. "Names correct?"

Both Clint and Tommy said yes.

"Okay, Tommy—are you called Tommy or Tom?"

"Either one is okay," Tommy said. He was looking down, and Clint could tell he was scared.

"Tell me what happened, Tom," Officer Mann.

"I already told Sheriff Logan," Tommy said. "He's the one who came when Eric called for help."

"I know you did, but I wasn't there and I'd like to hear it for myself."

Tommy drew a deep, slightly unsteady breath. "We were afraid of being late for school because of finals, and took the shortcut over Cougar Pass."

"You and Eric."

"Yes. I was driving. I came around that hairpin curve—you know the one—and there was one of those minivans smack-dab in the middle of the road. I hit the brakes and so did she, and we—we collided."

"You hit an icy spot."

"Frost. It was only melted where the sun, uh, shone on the road."

"Did you see that the driver was a woman?"

"Didn't have time to see anything. I was trying to straighten out my truck."

"Understandable."

"The van went off the road." Tommy swallowed hard. "I got the truck stopped, and Eric and I ran to the edge of the ravine. It was still going down, rolling end over end. We saw the woman fly out through the driver's door and land on the rocks. The van landed upside down about a foot from the river. We hurried down the grade as fast as we could. Eric thought she was dead, but I found a strong pulse and realized she was just knocked out. I told Eric to get back to the truck and go for help. He was about to leave when he spotted the fire. The woman was too close to the wreck, and I started thinking about, uh, maybe it would explode, you know? Eric didn't want to move her, but I knew we had to."

Tommy raised stricken eyes to look at Officer Mann. "We *had* to move her—she would have died in the explosions if we hadn't—but what if we hurt her more?"

"Tom, you did the right thing," Mann said. "She's alive and she wouldn't be if you'd left her where she was. Okay,

I have a few questions. Did she come to at all and say anything?"

"No."

"Did you happen to notice the license plate on the van?"

Tommy frowned. "I don't remember one."

"Then again, you might have been too occupied with other things to notice."

"That's true. It's just that the van's back end was toward us, but I can't remember a plate."

"It might have been thrown off during the tumble."

Tommy nodded. "That's possible, I guess."

"Where is this leading?" Clint asked.

"Have you seen the wreckage?" Officer Mann inquired.

"No."

"Well, there isn't any, other than a widespread ground cover of tiny pieces of fabric and metal and other unidentifiable debris." Mann sat back in his chair. "We don't know who she is. If Tommy had seen a license plate, we'd at least know in which state she lives."

"Lots of stuff fell in the river," Tommy said.

"Yes, but the river's running high and wild in that canyon from spring runoff. Everything's probably miles downstream by now."

"You're concerned about her identity," Clint said. "Won't that question be cleared up when she comes to?"

Officer Mann put away his notebook and pen. "I'm sure it will." He got to his feet and looked at Tommy. "That should do it for now. If any other questions come up that I think you might be able to answer, I'll contact you."

Tommy nodded. "Yes, sir."

Clint sensed Tommy's relief after the officer had gone. Neither Clint nor his son had ever been involved in anything that required police intervention, and Clint knew his son well enough to also know that that aspect of the accident made him nervous.

He put his hand on Tommy's shoulder. "Relax, son, Officer Mann is merely doing his job."

Tommy didn't answer, just kept staring across the room as though his father hadn't said a word.

Clint drew his hand back. He loved his son more than life itself, and felt his misery in his own soul. Tommy had never given him one moment of justified concern. Yes, Clint had worried some when Tommy began driving those mountain roads, but throughout the boy's life, Clint had been concerned for his safety, not because he had been misbehaving.

Clint changed the subject, simply to get Tommy thinking about something else. "When I called the principal and explained the situation, he said you could make up the tests you missed today." He paused, then added, "Guess I already told you that."

"That's okay, Dad."

"At least Eric didn't miss a full day." Clint frowned slightly. "How'd he get from the accident site to school?"

"When he called the sheriff, he also called his dad. Mr. Schulze picked him up." Tommy suddenly leaned forward and put his hands over his eyes. His voice broke. "It was awful, Dad. I'll never forget it."

Clint rubbed his son's back. "Of course you won't forget it. But you did everything you could to save that woman's life. I'm very proud of you, son. I hope you know that." He felt Tommy's shoulders heave with a sob, and he continued rubbing his back, doing what he could to comfort his boy.

There was no question of leaving the hospital and going home. Whatever they were finally told about the woman's condition, both he and Tommy had to hear it, firsthand and from a doctor. They had already occupied this little waiting room for five hours; they would remain right here for what was left of the day, and all night, if necessary.

* * *

At eight o'clock that evening nurse Nancy Cummings summoned Dr. Melvin Pierce to room 217. "She's showing signs of consciousness, Doctor."

Dr. Pierce glanced at the monitor screen that displayed the patient's heart rate and blood pressure. "Appears so," he murmured, and turned his attention to the woman in the bed. There were abrasions, cuts and scrapes on her face and hands. The gash on her right temple had required stitches, but X rays and other tests had revealed no broken bones, and even her concussion was not severe. In his opinion, she was extremely fortunate to have survived such a fierce accident with so little bodily damage.

He laid his hand on her upper arm and shook it slightly. "Miss? Miss, can you hear me? Open your eyes. You're in a hospital and I'm Dr. Pierce. Try to open your eyes."

As though from a very great distance, Sierra heard a man's voice. *Open your eyes. Try to open your eyes.*

Her eyelids felt weighted down by something heavy. Her entire body ached, especially her head. The palms of her hands burned as though on fire, her knees as well. She tried to think and couldn't.

But she heard the voice, and it seemed to be getting closer. She struggled to obey it, and finally her lids fluttered open. She saw a blurred face, and heard, "Miss, can you speak? Say something. Tell us your name."

Her brain felt stuffed with cotton. Her eyes closed, and she heard the voice again. "Try to stay awake, miss. Try to speak. What is your name?"

"Sierra," she mumbled thickly, and fell back into that dark place where her body didn't hurt and voices could not be heard.

Dr. Pierce straightened up and moved to the foot of the bed for her chart, on which he wrote the time and what had just occurred.

"Watch her closely," he said to the nurse as he wrote.

"I'll be leaving the hospital in about thirty minutes. Dr. North will be on duty. Call him if she awakens again."

He swung out of the room and strode directly to the ICU waiting room. Clint Barrow and his son stood up with expectant expressions.

"Go ahead and sit down again," the doctor said. He sat as well. He looked tired and rubbed his eyes with the heels of his hands. "Okay, here's what we know with some degree of certainty. She has a mild concussion and numerous abrasions. There are no broken bones, nor any detectable internal injuries. We do not count her as completely out of danger, but the outlook is favorable. She came to a few minutes ago for about ten seconds, and the fact that she understood what I was saying to her is an excellent sign. I asked her name and she said Sierra."

Clint and Tommy looked at each other. "Sierra? That was all she said?" Clint asked.

"The only word." Dr. Pierce got up. "I have other patients to see. My advice to the two of you is to go home and get some rest. The only thing you're going to accomplish here is to exhaust yourselves. Good evening." He left.

Tommy looked puzzled. "Isn't Sierra a peculiar name? Sounds more like a last name than a first. What do you think, Dad?"

"I don't know what to think about that, Tommy. But the rest of what Dr. Pierce said is very good news." He got to his feet. "Come on, I'll walk you out. It's time you went home. You have those exams to deal with tomorrow."

Tommy rose. "You're not going with me? How come?"

"I'm not sure. I just have this feeling that I should stick around."

"But you won't have a car."

"If I need a car, I'll rent one."

In the parking lot, Clint saw his son off. "Drive safely, and no shortcut over Cougar Pass."

Tommy nodded grimly. "Don't worry about that."

Clint watched the red pickup until it was out of sight, then walked back into the hospital. In ICU, he went directly to the nurse's station.

"May I see the woman in room 217?"

Nurse Cummings looked sympathetic. "She's still unconscious, Mr. Barrow."

"I know, and I would only stay a minute. But I need to see her, ma'am."

"Well…guess a little peek wouldn't hurt. Sure, Mr. Barrow, go ahead. Just don't touch anything."

"I won't. Thank you."

Clint walked down the corridor, hesitated a moment at the open door, then took a few steps into the room, which was lighted by one wall lamp. There was one bed, one patient, a woman who had said one word when asked her name. He winced at the stitches on her forehead and the mean-looking abrasions on her face and hands. There was a hospital cap on her head, but a bit of dark hair showed around the elastic. Her features were as close to perfect as he'd ever seen on a woman's face—small nose and chin, high cheekbones, well-defined eyebrows and full, beautifully sculpted lips.

"She's young," he muttered under his breath. For some reason he'd been thinking of her as a much older woman.

She looked small in that bed, which touched him, and the fact that she was hooked up to several machines touched him even more. An IV ran into her left arm, dripping a clear liquid into her veins.

His hands clenched into fists at his sides as he questioned why things like this had to happen. Tommy didn't deserve what he was going through, and neither did this woman.

A hundred thoughts ran through Clint's mind, but one stood out: he could not desert her. Until her full name was known and her relatives—there must be some—knew where she was and what had happened to her, he would assume familial responsibility and keep a sharp eye on her.

"Sierra," he whispered. "Is that really your name, or was your mind merely wandering?"

He looked at her for another few moments, sighed deeply and quietly left the room, returning to the nurse's station to speak to Nurse Cummings again.

"There's a little motel just down the block—the Bixby. Would you please call me there if there's any change in her condition, either good or bad?"

"Yes, Mr. Barrow, I'll call."

"Thank you. I'll probably be back in a few hours."

With her eyes still shut, Sierra mentally bemoaned the hardness of the bed she was lying in. Why was she in such an uncomfortable bed? She moved in an attempt to get more comfortable, and an onslaught of pain made her gasp. Her eyes flew open.

The room was unfamiliar—small, dimly lighted and austere. The door was wide open. *Where was she?* Panic seized her, and she tried to sit up, only to cry out in pain and fall back to the bed again. She saw the IV tube attached to her wrist. What was happening to her?

She swallowed, or tried to. Her throat and mouth were dry; her heart was pounding fearfully. Nurse Cummings rushed into the room and to the bedside, followed by another nurse.

"You're awake. Janie, call Dr. North," she said to the second nurse, who immediately hurried out. Then she smiled at Sierra. "How are you feeling, dear?"

"Could...could I have some water?" Sierra croaked.

"Certainly. There's some right here on your stand." The nurse produced a plastic glass of water with a straw. "Don't raise your head. I'll hold the glass for you. And take just a little this first time. Dr. North will be along in a moment."

Sierra sucked some water through the straw, then lay

back weakly. "Thank you," she whispered. "Where am I?"

"You're in a hospital, dear."

"Why?"

"Because of your injuries, of course. Oh, here's Dr. North." Nurse Cummings moved aside for the doctor, saying for his ears alone, "She seems a bit disoriented."

"Hello," Dr. North said, bending over her with an ophthalmoscope. "Look at the far corner of the room, please."

Sierra recoiled. "What are you doing?"

"This is an instrument that permits me to see the inside of your eyes."

"Why do you want to see the inside of my eyes?"

"Miss, uh, Sierra, you received a mild concussion in the accident. Examining your eyes is merely—"

"What accident?" Sierra cried, panicking again. "And why are you calling me Sierra?"

"Because you told another doctor that Sierra is your name." Dr. North's eyes narrowed thoughtfully. "Suppose you tell *me* your name."

Sierra's eyes darted wildly from doctor to nurse and then around the room. Her name...her name. Her head throbbed as she struggled to locate memories that weren't there. The void in her mind frightened her so much that she tried to get up again, driven by a need to escape this place, these people.

Dr. North pushed her down again and said to the nurse, "Whatever sedative Dr. Pierce prescribed for this patient, get it now!"

"Yes, Doctor." Nurse Cummings ran from the room and collided with Clint. "Excuse me, Mr. Barrow," she said, and rushed away.

"Excuse me, ma'am. What's going on?" he called after her. She didn't slow down, nor did she attempt to give him an answer. Frowning, Clint stepped into the room. Dr. North was attempting to stop the woman in the bed from thrashing around. She was emitting a low, keening sound and fighting to elude his restraint.

He strode to the opposite side of the bed. "What's wrong with her?" he anxiously asked.

The doctor glanced at him. "Who're you, and what are you doing here at three in the morning?"

"I'm Clint Barrow. My son Tommy was the driver of the other vehicle. Why is she so upset?"

"I think because I asked her her name."

"It's Sierra." Clint reached out and gently took her hand. "Sierra?" he said quietly. "Rest easy, Sierra, no one's is going to hurt you."

To Dr. North's amazement, she stopped fighting him. Her eyes went to Clint in a blank but much calmer stare. Taking a breath, Dr. North released his hold on her shoulders.

"You don't know me, Sierra," Clint said in that same even, quiet voice. "But I'm here to help you."

Sierra tried to focus her blurred vision on the man's face, but his features really didn't matter, his voice did. It was so kind and soothing, and she wanted to hear more of it.

Nurse Cummings returned with a syringe. "Here you are, Doctor."

"We may not need that, after all," he said in an undertone. He backed away from the bed and beckoned the nurse to a corner of the room. "She's responding to this man's voice," he said in a near whisper. "I want to see where it leads. You may go, I'm going to sit in here for a while."

"Yes, Doctor."

Clint was aware of Dr. North sitting out of Sierra's line of vision, but only vaguely, as he was focused on her and what he should say next.

Then instinct told him that she wouldn't care what he said as long as he kept talking. "I'm staying in the Bixby Motel. It's down the street a block or so. I awoke about an hour ago and decided I needed to see you again. I stopped in an all-night diner for something to eat, then came on over.''

''Where am I?'' she asked in a thin, wispy voice.

''In a hospital in Missoula, Montana. It's a very good hospital, Sierra. You are receiving the best care possible. Have you been hospitalized before?''

She lay silent and staring, and in the corner of the room Dr. North held his breath awaiting her answer.

It finally came, a very weak, very frightened, ''I...don't know.'' Dr. North noiselessly breathed again. He now knew what the patient's problem was.

Clint, however, was at a loss and could only rely on that instinct to keep talking to her. ''I was hospitalized once, Sierra, about ten years ago. A horse threw me and I landed wrong. Broke three ribs and—''

She interrupted. ''Who are you?''

''Name's Clint Barrow. Sierra—''

''Is Sierra my name? What's my last name? Do I live in Missoula?'' It was all said in a whispery, shaky voice.

Clint was finally catching on. He darted a glance at Dr. North, who responded with a nod. Sierra had amnesia. She remembered nothing, not even her name.

Clint's stomach sank, and he licked his suddenly dry lips. He was in over his head here. How much should he tell her? Should he mention the accident, explain what had happened to her, tell her that her van had been totally destroyed and that no one, not one single person in this hospital, maybe even in Missoula, knew who she was?

He mustered an unsteady smile. ''Now, that's information you're going to have to tell me. You see, I'm merely a concerned friend.''

''You're a friend. I see,'' she whispered, and Clint knew that her cloudy mind was placing him as an *old* friend, even though it was an illogical conclusion when he had just told her he had no answer to her questions.

Dr. North rose and approached the bed. "Perhaps we should let Sierra get some rest now, Mr. Barrow."

Her eyes became wild again and she clung to Clint's hand. "Don't leave," she begged him. "Please don't leave me alone."

"May I leave you alone for five minutes?" he asked gently. "I promise I'll be right back." He *had* to speak to the doctor alone.

"I...do you promise?" she whispered.

"You have my word." Gently he disengaged his hand and strolled from the room, knowing Dr. North would follow. They walked down the corridor and stopped in a quiet nook. Clint's eyes bored into the doctor's. "She can't remember anything, can she?"

"That appears to be the case. Mr. Barrow, her injuries were not sufficient to permanently destroy her memory. I will, naturally, order more extensive testing in the morning, but I honestly do not feel her loss of memory is physically caused. Trauma such as she went through in the accident can result in any number of emotional side effects. I strongly believe her amnesia is temporary."

"How temporary? Are we talking a few days, a week, a month?"

"I'm sorry, but there's no way of knowing. I find her response to you quite remarkable. You didn't know her before this?"

"No, we never met. Let me ask you something. How much should I tell her? I mean, should I talk about the accident?"

Dr. North thought for a moment. "My opinion is to avoid that topic for tonight. Talk in generalities. You were doing very well, and I think I'd keep conversation on that level until a psychologist sees her. I'll arrange for one to visit her first thing in the morning."

Clint was not normally a nervous man, but he was nervous about this. Why did Sierra trust him? What if he inadvertently said the wrong thing and sent her into another tizzy?

He took a long breath. "I'd better get back to her. Are you going to be available if something happens I can't handle?"

"I'll be here until 6:00 a.m. Call the nurse if you need me, and she will take it from there."

Clint returned to room 217 and saw that Sierra had a death grip on the safety rail on each side of her bed. Forcing a smile, he walked over to her. "Told you I'd be right back. Let's lower that rail, and then I'm going to move a chair over here so I can sit next to you."

Sierra watched his every move. She was so grateful he'd come back that tears stung her eyes. When he was seated and holding her hand again, she released a long, heavy sigh and closed her eyes.

"Thank you," she whispered, and fell asleep.

Clint stayed right where he was, and he was glad he had, because every ten minutes or so she woke up and looked at him briefly, as though subconsciously needing assurance that he was still there. Then she closed her eyes again.

Actually, he was damned glad she was sleeping at all, as he couldn't help worrying about further conversation with her.

Watching her sleeping and holding her hand was a bonding experience, he realized. She wasn't just the other half of Tommy's accident anymore, nor merely the woman in room 217, she was a flesh and blood human being with a troubled mind and the warmest, softest hand he had ever held.

He turned it once, looked at the abrasions on her palm and became choked up. The physical evidence of the accident would heal and vanish. Would the emotional damage heal and vanish, as well? Dr. North believed her amnesia was temporary.

All Clint could do was pray he was right.

Three

The next time Sierra awoke, her mind wasn't nearly as fuzzy as it had been. She knew she was in a hospital room. She remembered Dr. North and some nurses, and the man, Clint Barrow.

Turning her head slightly, she studied him. He had fallen asleep in a chair next to her bed. She recalled him saying they were friends, but friendship had many degrees. Were they merely speaking acquaintances, or were they much more? Frustration suddenly attacked her, and she brought her hand up to her head—perhaps to smooth her hair, or to nervously run her fingers through it, she really didn't know. But instead of feeling her abundant, heavy, straight hair, she discovered the cap covering it.

Why was she wearing a cap? Why couldn't she remember being brought to the hospital? *Why couldn't she remember her own name?*

"Oh, my God," she whispered as understanding developed. Her memory was gone! Her heart fluttered in panic.

Who was she? Where did she live? What had happened to cause so many aches in her body?

A nurse rushed in and saw that her patient was wide awake, the reason her heart rate had increased. She smiled and checked the flow of the IV. "Are you feeling all right, dear?"

Clint woke and sat up in the chair. "Sorry, I didn't intend to doze off. Is anything wrong?"

"Everything appears to be just fine," the nurse said brightly. "Our patient woke up, that's all."

Clint leaned toward the bed. "Are you all right, Sierra?" he asked softly.

She turned teary eyes to him. "I can't remember anything," she whispered.

The nurse patted her arm. "Dr. North said it's only temporary, dear. Try not to worry. You're doing fine."

"I have so many cuts and scrapes," Sierra said in a tear-clogged voice. "What happened? Why am I wearing a cap?"

"You have very long hair, dear," the nurse said. "The cap is merely a means to restrain it."

"But...my temple. Am I feeling stitches?" Sierra's hand was exploring her forehead.

"Don't touch them. There's no bandage, and we shouldn't risk infection."

Clint could tell that Sierra's mind was much clearer than it had been. She was going to ask questions—she had *already* asked questions—and he decided then and there that if the nurse didn't answer them, he would. Maybe a psychologist should talk to her first, but there wasn't one in the room, and to his way of thinking, she had every right to know what had happened to her.

Sierra asked nothing of the nurse, however. She accepted a drink of water, and lay still while the nurse checked the monitor connections.

"Well, everything seems to be in good order," the nurse

said briskly. "I'll be at the station if you need me." Her soft-soled shoes made very little sound as she left the room.

The second they were alone Sierra turned pleading eyes to Clint. "You said we're friends. Please tell me everything you know about me. Everything," she repeated in a choked voice.

He had no intention of refusing, although he wondered how best to explain that their friendship had begun only hours ago. If that information upset her…? It *would* upset her, Clint realized uneasily. She regarded him as her one connection with her past, perhaps as the key that would unlock the door to her memory.

This was far more of a burden than he'd bargained for, but he couldn't lie to her. "I am your friend, Sierra," he said quietly. "But I'm a new friend. We only met…recently."

"But you do know who I am."

Was he hearing panic in her voice again, seeing it in her eyes? He reached for her hand, and she let him hold it.

"Sierra, I'm not going to lie to you," he said. "You wouldn't want to hear anything but the truth, would you?"

"Is the truth something terrible?"

"It's limited, but not terrible."

"Tell me," she whispered.

He took a breath. "Here's what I know about you. You were in a car accident on a mountain road. My son was the driver of the other vehicle, a red pickup truck. You were driving a blue minivan. The road still had patches of early morning frost…."

She was staring at him so intently that he began to hope. "Is any of this familiar?"

She sounded discouraged as she answered, "No, but please go on. Was—was your son injured?"

"No, he wasn't."

"I'm glad."

"So am I, Sierra, so am I." Clint drew a breath before

continuing. "There was another young man in the truck
with Tommy, his friend Eric. They notified the sheriff and
you were brought to Missoula and this hospital by a flight-
for-life helicopter."

She tried to make a little joke. "My first helicopter ride
and I can't remember it."

*How did she know that helicopter ride had been her
first? Or was she merely assuming?*

Clint smiled for her benefit. "But you will remember it,
Sierra—that's what you've got to hang on to. Dr. North
told me he's positive your amnesia is temporary." Clint
paused to mentally go over that conversation. Had Dr.
North used the word *positive?*

Well, Clint couldn't backtrack now and shatter the little
hope he'd just given Sierra.

"And that's how we met," she said in a wispy, disappointed voice. "Because of your son. You really don't
know me much better than I know myself."

"I'm sorry, Sierra. I wish I could lay out your background in great detail, but I can't."

"My vehicle should offer some clues to my identity. I
must have had a driver's license with me. Do you know if
the police are checking that out?"

It was encouraging that she knew about driver's licenses,
but still Clint swallowed hard. Her question was one he
hated answering. In fact, he was afraid of answering it. She
would learn soon enough that the van and everything in it
had been destroyed.

He hedged, telling no lies, but deliberately avoiding the
whole truth. "The highway patrol is working on it."

"When did the accident happen?" she asked. "I—I'm
afraid I've lost track of time."

"Yesterday."

"Then they could very well know something today."
Sierra felt a surge of relief, certain once she knew her full
name and address, things would fall into place in her be-

fuddled brain. In the next heartbeat, however, she became doubtful again. If she'd had a driver's license with her, why didn't the hospital staff know her identity?

Her mouth became almost too dry to speak. "How do *you* know my first name is Sierra?"

"It's the name you gave a doctor when you came to the first time."

"I don't remember doing that," she murmured with a frown. "But why did anyone have to ask? I mean, if I had a driver's license—"

Clint hurriedly interrupted, steering the conversation in another direction. "Do you remember my name?"

"Yes, Clint Barrow. Do you live in Missoula?"

"My son and I live on our ranch. It's about eighty miles from Missoula. My wife passed away five years ago, so it's just Tommy and me."

"Oh, I'm sorry." Sighing heavily, Sierra moved her gaze from Clint to the ceiling above her bed. "I feel so...unconnected. Where was I going? Where had I come from?"

"I wish I knew, Sierra. The road you were on led to Cougar Mountain. The accident occurred in a place called Cougar Pass. It's very isolated country."

"And I was alone?"

"Yes, alone."

"I must have had a destination in mind. Your ranch is in that area, so there must be others. Maybe...maybe I was on my way to see someone."

Clint readily understood her need for information, and the speculation that need was inspiring, but letting her think that road held any answers would be more cruel than helpful.

"Sierra, I'm sorry, but no one lives on that road. It leads to only one thing—Cougar Mountain. It's a place that draws mountain climbers, hikers, environmentalists and campers seeking isolation."

To his surprise, her countenance brightened. "Then I must be one of them!" she exclaimed. "The clues to who I am are in my van, I know they are. Even though everyone involved obviously missed finding my driver's license, this is very encouraging. Would you happen to know where my van is now? I mean, was it towed somewhere?"

Clint was so glad to see Dr. North walking in at that moment he could have kissed him.

"Wide awake, I see," the doctor said with a big smile. "Mr. Barrow, would you leave us alone for a few minutes? It's nearly six and I'll be leaving the hospital soon, but I'd like to examine my favorite patient before I go."

Clint immediately rose in deference to the doctor's wishes, but Sierra wouldn't release his hand. And when he looked into her beautiful dark eyes, he saw a resurgence of panic.

"Don't leave me," she begged.

"I'll wait just outside the door," Clint promised.

Biting her upper lip, not quite succeeding in maintaining dry eyes, she reluctantly let go of Clint's hand. He barely breathed until he was in the corridor outside her room. Never had he felt another person's emotions as strongly as he felt Sierra's. He was shaken through and through, and more than a little panicked himself.

Hurrying to the waiting room, he purchased coffee from a machine, then returned to the corridor to drink it and wait for Dr. North to complete his examination. The coffee was strong and hot and tasted good. Leaning against a wall, he drank it while pondering Sierra's trust of him.

Dr. North finally came out. Clint pushed away from the wall. "I need to talk to you."

Nodding, the doctor walked down the corridor with him. "Physically she seems to be doing very well," Dr. North began. "But to be a little more certain than we are at this time, I've scheduled some additional tests for this morning.

Also, Dr. Trugood, a psychologist, will be seeing her around nine.''

"I know you're doing everything medically possible for her, Doctor, but she's asking questions that are damned hard to answer.''

"Mr. Barrow, her state of mind is only natural in amnesia patients. I find her emotional dependency on you, a stranger, rather interesting, as I think Dr. Trugood will.''

"Is it unusual?''

"Frankly, I haven't worked with amnesiacs enough to know. Dr. Trugood should be able to answer that question, however.''

"I guess what I'm getting at is you told me to avoid talking about the accident, which was impossible to do. She might not remember her past, but she's a very bright woman and she's digging for answers. Plus she's positive that the things she had in the van with her—driver's license, for instance—will reveal her identity. I told her about the accident—I had to—but I haven't told her about the van and everything in it being destroyed.''

"I see,'' Dr. North said thoughtfully. "I hesitate to instruct you not to return to her room, when you promised her you would, but if she's counting on learning her identity from the contents of her vehicle, and you tell her there's no way that's going to happen…'' The physician frowned and stopped walking.

"This really must be left to Dr. Trugood,'' he said after a few moments. "What I'd like you to do is go back to her room and tell her that work, duty, family responsibility, something—use your own judgment on that—demands that you leave the hospital for a while. Assure her that you will return.'' Dr. North cocked an eyebrow. "Assuming that you plan to return, of course.''

Clint's mind raced. He felt the same mysterious bond with Sierra that she apparently felt with him. He didn't understand it, but it was a driving force that he knew he couldn't ignore.

"I'll be back," he said with a touch of grimness in his voice. "How about this evening?" he asked, thinking that he could call the ranch and have one of his men drive to Missoula and pick him up. It was a good idea, because he could then drive back in his own vehicle. Also, he wanted to see with his own eyes how Tommy was doing.

"I think this evening would work out perfectly," Dr. North said. "She'll be through with the tests and she'll have talked to Dr. Trugood."

"Will he tell her about the loss of her possessions?"

"I'll call him and suggest that he does."

"Well, someone's got to do it," Clint said rather sharply. "If she doesn't know by tonight, I'll have to tell her."

"I understand. I'm sure Dr. Trugood will take care of it." Dr. North glanced at his watch. "I have to be going. We'll talk again."

Clint watched the doctor stroll down the corridor toward the elevators, then he turned and headed back to Sierra's room. His heart was in his throat. He was a simple man, and the situation was so far from simple it was almost laughable. At the door to Sierra's room, he took a calming breath and erased the grimness from his face. When he stepped into the room he was wearing a smile. With his own eyes he saw the tension leave Sierra's body.

"Clint," she said with unabashed relief, holding her hand out to him.

He moved closer and took it. "You were worried I wouldn't be back. Sierra, when I tell you something you can bank on it, okay?"

"Okay," she whispered.

"There's something I have to tell you now. I'm going to have to leave you until this evening." He felt her hand stiffen in his and saw the fear in her eyes. "There are things

I have to take care of," he said, standing firm although he felt as though his heart was breaking.

"Work?" she said in that whispery, frightened little voice with which he'd become so familiar.

Clint nodded. "Work and other things. You'll see me again no later than eight tonight." There were tears in her eyes, and he took a tissue from the box on the stand and gently blotted the escaping moisture, carefully keeping away from her stitches and abrasions.

"You have every right to cry," he said softly. "I'm not going to tell you to keep a stiff upper lip and a lid on your emotions. Sometimes a good cry is very good medicine."

"It—it isn't that I want to cry," she said brokenly. "I just can't seem to help it."

"And it's fine with me. Never feel that you should hold anything back with me, Sierra."

She blinked at the tears and attempted a shaky smile. "I feel so different with you than with anyone else. I wish I knew why." She sighed then. "There's so much I wish I knew."

"You will. Try to hold that thought." On impulse Clint leaned over the bed and gently pressed his lips to the un-injured portion of her forehead. This woman, helpless and bewildered, and known only as Sierra, touched him deeply. She needed him, was relying on him, and he vowed not to let her down. He straightened up and forced himself to smile. "See you this evening, all right?"

"Yes, this evening," she whispered, and let her hand slip from his as he left the bed and then the room. Alone, she darted her eyes around the room. There were no demons in the early morning shadows, nothing to fear, and yet fear was an enormous part of her when Clint wasn't holding her hand. She believed what he told her much more readily than she did the doctors and nurses. Did he remind her of someone she knew and couldn't remember? Someone who was kind and gentle and completely honest?

She lay there and thought about Clint Barrow. He was a handsome man, or at least she saw him as handsome. His looks didn't matter, however; his kindness, thoughtfulness and consideration did. He was probably a wonderful father to his son, caring, loving and genuinely interested in anything Tommy did or said.

Did she have a father somewhere? A mother? Maybe a...husband? She adjusted her position, tried to ignore the additional discomfort movement caused, and looked closely at her left hand. She wore no jewelry, but there was a faint indentation on her ring finger that indicated she'd worn a ring for some time.

It could be a clue! Anxiously she pushed the nurse's call button. A young woman came almost at once. "Yes, ma'am?"

"Was I wearing a ring when I was brought in?" Sierra asked.

"I wouldn't know, ma'am. But I'll check your admission slip and find out, if you'd like."

"Please. You see, my finger looks as though I've been wearing a ring." Although the IV was in her left wrist, Sierra lifted that hand from the bed.

The young nurse peered at it. "Yes, you're right. I'll go and see what I can find out."

Sierra felt excitement coursing through her system. A husband could mean children. A family would certainly be looking for her. But if she had a family, why had she been traveling alone?

Her head started aching more than it already had been. Closing her eyes, she breathed deeply and fought impatience, doubt, frustration....

Footsteps announced the young nurse's return. Sierra's eyes flew open. "Did you learn anything?"

"Your admission slip lists only a watch."

"No ring?" Intense disappointment gripped Sierra.

"I'm very sorry. You were counting on a ring, weren't you?"

"I...guess so."

"Is there anything else, ma'am? Breakfast will be served shortly, and then you'll be given a bath. A bath always makes a person feel better."

"Thank you," Sierra said dully.

Clint was waiting in the yard when Tommy drove in from school. "Dad," the teenager exclaimed as he jumped out of his truck. "How'd you get home?"

"I had Lyle drive in and pick me up. How are you doing, Tom?"

"Okay, I guess. I think I did all right on the exams today."

"That's good." Clint studied his son's face and eyes and felt relief; Tommy's color was back to normal, and he seemed like his usual exuberant self.

Tommy reached into the truck for a book, which he held up with an exaggerated grimace. "Trig test tomorrow. Thought I'd better do a little boning up."

"Aren't you going to ask about Sierra?" Clint asked quietly.

"Uh, yeah, sure. Does—does she remember the accident?"

"She doesn't remember anything, Tom. I spent quite a lot of time with her, and I told her what happened. She seems to trust me."

"Yeah, well, you're a trustworthy guy, Dad," Tommy quipped. "I'm starving. What's Rosie cooking for supper?"

"I'm not sure. Chicken, maybe." Clint felt a strange disappointment over Tommy's lack of interest in Sierra's progress. He'd thought Tom would be full of questions, and instead he hardly seemed concerned. For a young man who had shed tears over the death of a foal only two weeks ago, unconcern for a human being seemed greatly out of character.

"I've gotta get something to eat," Tommy said. "Are you coming in, Dad?"

"Not right now, Tom. You go ahead." While Tommy sprinted to the house, Clint walked over to a corral and leaned his forearms on the top rail. There were horses in the enclosure, but he didn't see them. A sense of something being not quite right gnawed at him, occupying his mind and wrenching his gut.

But never once had he not given Tommy the benefit of the doubt. Tommy was young, still only a boy, really, and maybe he *couldn't* dwell on the accident. Even though it had been no more his fault than Sierra's, it was possible that Tommy was suffering feelings he couldn't talk about.

Clint pushed away from the corral, thinking that must be it. It would be a first—he and Tommy had always been able to talk about anything—but "anything" before the accident had been topics without such serious ramifications. His best course would be to let Tommy deal with this in his own way and time, Clint decided. Tommy knew he was here for him, and that was really what was most important.

When Clint approached the open door to Sierra's room that evening, he first saw the empty bed, then her still form sitting in a chair near the window. It was dark outside, but her face was turned to the glass. The cap was gone from her head, and he registered the rich, dark color of her hair, its marvelous length secured at her nape with something red.

He thought of that for only a moment, though, as he was so pleased to find her out of bed. He stepped into the room. "Sierra?"

Her head came around. The forlorn, lost expression on her face tore at his heartstrings. Hastily he crossed the small room and knelt beside her chair. "What's wrong, Sierra?" he asked gently.

"There is no driver's license," she said dully. "There's nothing. My van was completely destroyed in the accident. A police officer came by to speak to me today, and he told me everything. Did you know?"

"Yes, but the doctors didn't think it was my place to tell you about it." Self-recrimination thinned his lips. He should have gone with his own instincts and told her himself. "Would it have been easier to hear, coming from me?"

She lowered her eyes. "I don't know. Maybe." Sighing, she looked at him again. "I'm glad to see you. Thank you for coming back."

"I told you I would."

"I know, but the day was so…awful, it wouldn't have surprised me if you hadn't." She fashioned a weak smile. "I don't think the doctors know what to do with me. Every test was normal. A psychologist dropped in twice, once this morning and again this afternoon after the results of the tests came in. He said…to relax. He said my memory would clear up much faster if I relaxed and let it happen."

"You sound doubtful."

"I sound tense, Clint, because I *am* tense. How can I relax? How could anyone in my situation? I can't help trying to remember. It's all I think about. I asked the police officer if anyone had turned in a missing person report for someone of my description. No one has, not in this jurisdiction. Clint, I didn't just suddenly appear from another planet. *Someone* must be wondering where I am."

"Maybe it's too soon for relatives and friends to become alarmed. Have you considered that?"

Sierra was silent a moment. "That's the first really sensible thing anyone's said to me all day. You're right. Maybe I talked to friends and relatives just before the accident. Maybe I told them I would be out of touch for a

few days.'' Hope again shone in Sierra's eyes. "I should
have thought of that.''

Clint patted her arm and stood up. "At least you're out
of bed. I consider that major progress, Sierra.''

Her face fell again, startling him. "They're going to
move me out of ICU in the morning. Physically, I'm fine.
Everything's healing nicely, no infections, no complica-
tions. My doctors apparently went into a huddle after the
results of the test came through and decided I could go
home after a few more days.'' Her voice cracked. "Where
is home? Where will I go? I don't even have any clothes.''

"They're not going to just throw you out on the street,
Sierra.''

"I know. They mentioned...welfare.'' With an agonized
moan, she covered her face with her hands. "I can't bear
it, I can't! Maybe my mind is gone, but I know in my heart
that I never lived on welfare.''

"Your mind is *not* gone," Clint said sharply. "I've spent
enough time with you to know that you're an intelligent
woman. Sierra, there's no shame in accepting charity in a
situation like yours.'' As positive as he sounded in his attempt to bolster her spirit, he knew how she felt. A discomfiting picture formed in his mind—of Sierra living
alone in some little apartment, trying desperately to remember, living with hope one minute and despair the next, probably seeing the psychologist once or twice a week but staying pretty much to herself.

He couldn't let that happen to her. Again he knelt beside
her, this time taking her hand in his. "Listen to me. When
the hospital releases you, I'm going to take you to my
ranch. It's peaceful there, Sierra, quiet and beautiful. That's
where you're going to do your healing.''

She was blinking away tears. "But...I would be...a terrible imposition.''

"You most certainly will not be an imposition. The
house is huge, with three empty bedrooms. I have a house-

keeper and cook, Rosie Slovek, and you won't have to do one damned thing except rest and relax.''

"It...sounds wonderful.'' She smiled faintly. "Why are you so kind to me?''

"Because you don't deserve what happened to you. Neither does my son. He can't even bring himself to talk about the accident. Your presence on the ranch will be good therapy for him as well as for you. Say you'll come.''

"I will, of course I will. Oh, Clint.'' She surprised him by putting her arms around his neck and sobbing into his shirt.

He rubbed her back and made consoling noises, but he was very much aware of her breasts against his chest and her warm, womanly scent. Even with bruises and stitches discoloring her face, she was a beautiful woman, and he felt her in that most private and personal part of himself that had been latent since his wife's death.

It shook him that he could feel so much for a woman he barely knew. He wouldn't even attempt to give the feeling a name, although he was certain it wasn't caused by pity.

He cleared his throat and said, "Here now, it's nothing to cry over.''

Sierra pulled away and took a tissue from the pocket of her hospital robe. Wiping her eyes, she smiled wanly. "How will I ever repay you?''

"By getting well.'' There was a peculiar hoarseness in his voice, and he cleared his throat. "Just by getting well, Sierra.''

She nodded once.

Four

Clint awoke before dawn the next morning, which wasn't that far from normal. But the tight knot squeezing his gut wasn't at all normal, and he lay in bed and thought of all that had happened, and what part of it might be causing the discomfort he was feeling.

It struck him out of the blue: they were moving Sierra out of ICU this morning! No problem there; in fact it was an extremely good sign. But moving her where? Into a room with other patients? No way, he thought grimly, bounding out of bed and heading for the shower.

He was at the hospital in Missoula at eight and went directly to the administration wing, which was just becoming active for the day. It took a few minutes but he finally found someone of authority, an older woman who wore a plastic-covered card on her jacket that stated her name was Mrs. Marion Green. She agreed to speak with him and invited him into her office.

They sat down. ''What can I do for you, Mr. Barrow?''

"There's a woman in the hospital with amnesia, and all anyone knows about her is that her name might be Sierra," he began.

Mrs. Green nodded. "I'm aware of Sierra. Do you know her?"

"My son was the driver of the other vehicle. I've only known her since the accident. She's being moved from ICU this morning, and I want to make sure she's given a private room. I'm willing to take full financial responsibility for her care, and—"

Mrs. Green interrupted. "*You* intend to pay her bills?"

"Yes. Since her vehicle was completely destroyed in the accident, I have a feeling my insurance company is going to delay a settlement decision. Truth is, I haven't yet turned in a claim. My son's truck was only minimally damaged, and while I believe it was a no-fault accident, my insurance company might feel differently. I don't want Sierra bearing the brunt of bureaucratic red tape while they decide. She's going to be here only a few more days, and I want her in a private room."

"I see." Mrs. Green got up and went to a file cabinet for some forms. Seated again, she filled in blanks on the forms with a pen, then pushed them across the desk. "If you sign these papers, Mr. Barrow, the hospital and whatever doctors treated her will hold you financially responsible for Sierra's care." She laid her pen next to the forms.

Clint picked it up and scrawled his name at the bottom of each form. Standing, he said, "May I count on your discretion? I don't want anyone worrying Sierra with information she doesn't need to hear."

"You'd rather she not learn of your generosity?"

"That's right."

Mrs. Green gathered the forms. "It will not leave administration, Mr. Barrow. You have my word."

"Thank you." Clint left the administration wing, then the hospital itself. He had other plans for the morning and would be returning before noon. By then Sierra should be in her new room—her new *private* room.

Sierra brightened when Clint walked into her room. She had left the door open for him, positive one minute he would come, worried the next that he wouldn't. It wasn't that she doubted his word, but as hard as she tried to stay calm and unafraid when she was alone, she couldn't quite manage it. She felt better the second she saw him.

"Hello," Clint said, deliberately avoiding asking how she was feeling, as he figured she probably heard enough questions in that vein from the hospital staff.

He was carrying a large, colorful paper bag with handles, which he ignored while he looked around the room. The walls were painted a pretty peach hue, there was a television set and two chairs, and the drapes at the window were a cheerful garden of flowery colors. "Nice room," he said. "Do you like it?"

Sierra was sitting in one of the chairs. "I...think so. Yes," she quickly added, not wanting him to think she was a complainer. His friendship was so valuable to her, the most precious thing she possessed, and she wondered if she had always eluded negative opinions of herself from people she cared about, if that was her nature. "It's a very pleasant room."

Clint moved the other chair closer to hers and sat down. "I brought you something." He set the bag at her feet.

Without touching it she peered into the top of the sack and saw pink tissue paper. "You brought something for me?" She blinked to hold back the tears.

Clint sensed her emotion and, leaning forward, gently took her hand. "They're only things I thought you needed, Sierra. Take a look at them."

She realized that she would rather sit there with her hand in his. His eyes were so blue they were vibrant, and she studied his handsome face and the compassion and warmth of his expression. Had anyone ever been so kind to her before?

His gift was another sign of that kindness, and he wanted her to see it. Sliding her hand from his, she reached into the bag. It contained a soft white-and-pink robe, two cotton-knit nightgowns, one in pink, the other pale green, and a pair of bedroom slippers.

"Oh, they're beautiful," she said. "Clint, you shouldn't have. I've been doing just fine with the hospital gowns."

"A pretty woman needs pretty things to wear," he said. "I guessed at sizes, and if they don't fit I can exchange them."

Sierra was touched that he would call her pretty. She'd seen herself in a mirror and had examined the abrasions and discolored blotches on her face. It was possible she might be pretty when everything healed, but it would be awhile before that happened.

"Thank you. I'm sure they'll fit." Checking the labels, she saw that he'd purchased everything in a medium size. Her eyes suddenly jerked to his. "Clint, I haven't forgotten everything. I can read!"

He looked so pleased and she felt so excited that they each sat there and grinned. "I'll bet you can write, too. Have you tried it?" Clint said. He took a pen from his shirt pocket and held it out. "Use the sack."

Her hand shook slightly as she accepted the pen, but she wrote "Clint Barrow" on the sack, clearly and with a pretty flourish. "Is that how you spell your name?" she asked.

"Exactly," he said with another broad smile. "And don't forget that you knew about driver's licenses and missing person reports. You remember a lot more than we initially thought. You're going to be all right, Sierra."

For the first time since she'd become aware of her amnesia, she believed recovery was possible.

Sierra inhabited that room for three days. Dr. Trugood, the psychologist, dropped in every afternoon and chatted

with her. But as cleverly as he steered their conversations
to probe her memory, she still could not remember anything
prior to waking up in ICU.

It was a horrible feeling during the day, but at night,
alone in that pretty peach room after Clint had left, it was
worse than horrible. Her pulse would race and her head
would throb while she tried to remember something, anything—a face, a name, a place. Her mind wouldn't coop-
erate, and then the tears of frustration would begin.

She felt safe only when Clint was with her, and she could
hardly wait for the doctors to release her so she could go
home with him. He had told her so much about his ranch
that she had formed a picture of it in her mind, and she
was anxious to see if that image coincided with reality.

On the third evening of her stay in the peach room, Clint
arrived to see her walking the floor and smiling, actually
looking happy. "I can leave in the morning. They said
around ten," she exclaimed.

Clint already knew that, as an administrative assistant
had caught him on his way in. But he would not rain on
Sierra's parade and acted as though this was the first time
he'd heard her news.

"I'm very glad," he told her, and was surprised when
she moved closer to him and put her arms around him. It
was a hug of gratitude, nothing more, he told himself, and
he hugged her back, intending only to accept her way of
thanking him. The electricity he felt while holding her,
however, had nothing to do with gratitude. He closed his
eyes and savored the sensation. It had been a long time
since he'd held a woman like this, and the bond he already
felt with Sierra deepened and took on new meanings.

She stepped back and smiled up at him. "They laundered
the clothes I was wearing when I was brought in, so I'll
have something to wear tomorrow. When I think about it,
everyone's treated me so well. I asked Dr. Pierce about the

hospital bill, and he told me not to concern myself with it. Isn't that remarkable? Imagine them treating a patient pro bono.'' Sierra's eyes widened. ''My Lord, where did that term come from?''

''It's Latin. Do you know what it means?''

''I think it means for free. Clint, how would I know that?''

''You're beginning to remember things from the past,'' he said gently, marveling that he could sound so like his usual self when he was still feeling her body against his, still smelling her scent as though it had drilled itself into the very nucleus of his cells.

He took a long but quiet breath to clear his head. He would tell Tommy tonight that Sierra would be staying with them. Clint hadn't yet mentioned it to his son, and he wondered why. Maybe because Tommy had been so busy coming and going, and so had he. But even when there'd been opportunity, Tommy hadn't seemed to like talking about Sierra, though Clint had never attempted to conceal how often he visited her in Missoula.

Thinking of his son reminded him of something. ''Tommy's high school graduation ceremony is being held this coming Friday evening. You can go with me, if you'd like.''

Sierra's thoughts were still on that term *pro bono*. How strange that the first inkling of her past would be something like that. What did it mean? What *could* it mean?

Clint's invitation finally registered, and she found herself recoiling from the idea. She wasn't ready for a crowd of strangers, for perhaps hundreds of unfamiliar eyes looking at her. She suddenly felt choked and panicky, and stammered, ''Uh, if you wish,'' simply because she would do almost anything that Clint might suggest. For him, not for herself.

He saw the sudden fear in her dark eyes and understood it. Putting his hands on her shoulders, he said quietly, ''Sierra, you don't have to do anything that makes you uncomfortable." He didn't think it was healthy for her to hide on the ranch, but neither would he push her into leaving it before she was ready to do so.

Her voice became husky. "Why are you so good to me?"

He didn't know how to answer that question. Because of the accident? Because she'd been so alone and bereft? Out of a sense of decency and responsibility because Tommy had been involved? Because he had a natural tendency to help anyone in trouble? Maybe all those reasons, and more, had been the start of it, but now he was good to her because he truly cared for her.

A ripple of shock ran through Clint's system. Was it true? Did he have *those* kinds of feelings for a woman he knew next to nothing about?

"Sierra," he said, speaking evenly though it wasn't easy to do, "you needed *someone* to be good to you. Guess I just sort of volunteered for the job."

Apparently she accepted his reply, because he saw, with great relief, that she was smiling again.

"You're a good person," she said softly.

Before heading for the ranch the next morning, Clint drove to a shopping mall. Sierra looked at him questioningly as he pulled into a parking space.

"We're going to buy you some clothes," he said firmly.

"Clint, you can't! You've already done so much."

"How are you going to get by with one shopworn set of clothes? Sierra, I'm going to tell you something. My ranch has been in my family for four generations. I own it free and clear, and it makes money every year. I can well afford the cost of a new wardrobe for you. Now we're going inside that mall and I want you to buy anything you like without worrying about the price, okay?"

She heaved a heavy sigh and then said rather meekly,

"Okay." In the back of her mind, however, she made a promise to herself. She needed clothes, that was a given, but she would buy only the necessities.

If she could remember what was necessary and what wasn't, that is.

Shopping had never been a favorite pastime for Clint, but he found himself enjoying it with Sierra. Just being with her was a pleasure, he thought, while watching her go through a circular rack of blouses and shirts.

But he was catching on that she was looking only for plain, serviceable clothes, the more inexpensive the better, and he walked to the rack and pulled out a deep rose blouse.

"Do you like this one?" he asked her.

"It's beautiful, but it's very..." She stopped to clear her throat.

"You weren't going to say 'expensive,' were you?" Turning to the clerk, he handed her the blouse. "We'll take this one, if it fits, and—" he pulled out two others, one royal blue, the other emerald green "—these."

The clerk smiled. "You have a good eye. These jewel tones are perfect for your wife's coloring."

Startled, Sierra opened her mouth to deny the relationship, but Clint smoothly intervened before she could say anything. "Do you have slacks and skirts that match those blouses?"

As they followed the clerk to another area of the store, he made a silly face and grinned at Sierra. She couldn't help laughing, and the sound of her laughter was sweet music to Clint's ears. She made him feel young, he realized. He was thirty-nine years old but had felt much older for a very long time. Since Janine died, in fact—five lonely years ago. He'd been only thirty-four when his wife died, but he had almost immediately turned into an old man.

Clint sat on a chair to wait for Sierra to try on an armload of skirts, slacks, jeans and dresses, and pondered the changes in himself since meeting her. It wasn't difficult to pinpoint those changes: he felt alive again, as young as springtime when the sap rises in the trees, and vital, excited in a way he'd almost forgotten.

But he knew without question that it was not something he would tell Sierra. Who was she, really, other than the loveliest and warmest of women? She could be married, he thought with a sinking sensation.

His spirits sank even lower as the talk he'd had with Tommy last night came to mind. Tommy's intensely negative reaction to hearing that Sierra would be living at the ranch for an indefinite period had out-and-out shocked Clint. Why would the boy object so strenuously to Sierra's presence? Clint still couldn't figure it out, although he'd mulled it over for hours after going to bed. It had never once occurred to him that Tommy wouldn't want her living with them, and his son had to have a reason for feeling that way, even if *he* hadn't been able to get Tommy to tell him what it was.

It bothered Clint today that he'd finally ended the heated discussion by firmly stating, "She's coming. Get used to it!" It was not how he normally spoke to his son, and he'd seen the pinched look of defiance in Tommy's eyes as he'd stormed from the room.

This morning Tommy had left without breakfast. Clint had walked into the large country kitchen and Tommy had walked out. Rosie, who had worked on the ranch for so long she seemed to be part of the family, had asked, "What's wrong with that boy this morning?"

Clint had answered truthfully. "Sierra's being discharged today. I'm bringing her to the ranch because she has nowhere else to go, and for some reason that he won't talk about, Tommy doesn't like the idea. We had a falling out about it last night."

"Oh, goodness," Rosie had said with a troubled expression. "The two of you have always gotten along so well. I surely hate seeing a rift between you."

"I do, too, Rosie, but Tommy is old enough to understand that things can't always go his way."

"That he is," Rosie had murmured, but Clint could tell she was still troubled.

Well, so was he. He hated discord with his son. It happened so rarely that Clint couldn't even remember the last time there'd been bad feelings between them.

Regardless, he would not put up with any rudeness toward Sierra, and Tommy *had* to know him well enough to know that.

During the drive through the city to reach the highway that would ultimately take them to the Barrow Ranch, Sierra stared intently out the windows at everything—stores, houses, cars, people—with the hope of seeing something that would strike a familiar chord.

"I wonder if I've ever been in Missoula before," she murmured quietly, more to herself than to Clint.

He heard her, though. "I've wondered that same thing myself. What does it look like to you?

"It's a pretty town," she said slowly, after a moment's thought.

Clint pondered her comment. In Montana, Missoula was a city. Sierra saw it as a town. Could that be a clue to where she lived? Was her home in some large city? If so, she wasn't from Montana at all. There were no large cities in the state, nothing even close to Los Angeles or Denver, for instance.

He cast her a sidelong glance. She was a terrific woman. Look how she had gone into that mall without one vain comment about the sutures and scrapes on her face. Someone somewhere had to be wondering where she was. Why in God's name had she been heading for Cougar Mountain all by herself?

Of course, there were women who hiked alone in isolated areas, the same as some men did.

She was a puzzle, that was certain. What if the doctors were wrong and she *never* regained her memory?

"Oh, I almost forgot," Sierra said, interrupting Clint's uneasy thoughts. "Officer Mann came to see me this morning. He knew I was being discharged and wanted to talk about the accident before I left Missoula. Apparently he also knew you were going to pick me up."

She paused for a moment to wonder how the state patrol officer knew as much about herself as she did, then continued. "He has men scouring the place where the accident happened, picking up every piece of rubble, so experts may examine them. Apparently there are ways to identify a vehicle just from debris. Isn't that amazing?"

"What they're looking for, Sierra, is something with a number. VINs, or vehicle identification numbers, are stamped on various parts of every automobile manufactured. Then there are motor numbers, model numbers, all sorts of numbers, and one of those is what John Mann is hoping to find."

Sierra might not have a very long memory, but she could still reason. "And if they can identify my vehicle, they'll be able to identify its owner?"

"I think that's the idea," Clint confirmed.

"Officer Mann also asked for my fingerprints," Sierra said. "Naturally, I let him take them. He's a very thorough policeman, isn't he?"

Clint felt no small amount of alarm. John Mann would run her fingerprints through the FBI's computer, and what if law enforcement learned something about Sierra she'd be better off if they didn't know?

Not that he thought there was the remotest chance of Sierra having a criminal record, but... Damn, there were so many *buts* connected to Sierra! John Mann had taken advantage of her ignorance this morning, and Clint didn't like it.

There was nothing he could do about it now, though, except wish that he'd been there when the officer had requested Sierra's fingerprints. Clint sent her another glance, this one containing worry. She was so damned innocent of the ways of the world, so naive and vulnerable in her present state of mind.

She was wearing a pair of new jeans and the rose-colored blouse Clint had picked from the rack, and she looked radiantly beautiful. He never even saw the abrasions on her face anymore. Her glossy dark hair was nipped in at her nape with a pretty clip, something she had chosen herself. He recalled stopping her at a cosmetic counter in a large department store in the mall, and how she had said, "I don't wear makeup, Clint," without even realizing she had just given him another clue to the woman she really was. She had let him buy her some moisturizer and a lightly scented cologne at that counter, but that was all. She had then looked at him nervously and said, "I hate asking, but...I need some things that I haven't seen in the mall."

Of course, he'd thought, what was wrong with him? Women had special needs, which he should have thought of himself.

They had made one more stop, at a drugstore, and he'd given her some cash and waited in the truck for her to finish her shopping.

Now they were heading out of Missoula, and he could tell that she was avidly interested in the green fields, the small ranches on each side of the road and the more distant scenery, the mountains they were driving toward.

Something she'd said about John Mann's visit this morning flashed into Clint's mind. "They're gathering debris at the accident site for examination? Sierra, would you like to go there and see where the accident happened?"

Her breath suddenly caught, and her hand rose to splay at her throat. "Uh, if you wish."

"No, it's not what I wish. Would *you* like to see the site?"

She felt as though she should want to see it, and wondered why the idea was so unnerving. It was, terribly. She felt cold and clammy and scared to death.

Clint could tell she was having a hard time making a decision, and he intervened. "Let's not do it today. You're probably tired."

"I...yes, I do feel...rather tired."

"Shopping is hard work," Clint said lightly in an attempt to ease the discomfort he'd unwittingly caused her by mentioning the accident site.

Sierra's response was a weak little smile of gratitude that he would be so in tune with her feelings. She clutched at the change of topic. "You bought me so much more than I really needed, Clint. Those dresses, for instance." There was a canopy over the bed of Clint's pickup truck, and the space was almost full of packages and sacks and clothes on hangers protected by plastic covers. There were jackets, sweaters, shoes, lingerie, jeans and slacks, skirts and blouses, more nightclothes, plus two beautiful dresses and a coat to wear over them. Clint had even insisted she pick out hosiery, and ankle socks. If they had missed any component of a complete wardrobe, she couldn't imagine what it might be.

She *was* tired, she realized. Relieved to be out of the hospital, excited to be going to Clint's ranch, but still tired. Exhausted, really. Almost every minute of every hour for days now she'd been straining her mind to remember something, anything. But just recently she had learned that she could also bring herself to a place of utter peace, a place without hounding questions that had no answers, and while Clint said that she did need everything he'd bought for her, she put her head back and closed her eyes, seeking that wonderful serenity she had discovered.

Clint saw her resting and felt a heartrending tenderness for this beautiful, lost woman. On his life, he swore that he would be there for her for as long as she needed him, *however* she needed him.

As he drove he thought of many things, and it came to him that he'd been living only half a life since Janine's death. He hadn't realized it; he'd honestly thought everything was all right. He was a hard worker and usually worked with one crew or another on some portion of the ranch. He'd had Tommy to go home to at day's end. Not so much this last year, because Tommy was growing up, in his senior year, dating girls, spending time with his friends and talking, sporadically, about going away to college in the fall. He had applied at three universities and been accepted by each. He hadn't yet decided on one, but that decision had to be made very soon. Tommy knew it; Clint knew it. There were times when Tommy mentioned not going to college at all. The ranch had always been his home, and he wasn't keen on leaving it.

But Clint attributed those ambiguities to Tommy's hormonal ups and downs. Some days he was a man, and on others he was still a boy. Clint had always encouraged further education, as had Janine. They had met in college and gotten married a week after graduation. Clint knew how Tommy's horizons would expand with college. New friends, a wider understanding of the world in general, increased confidence. But Clint wouldn't force, or try to force, Tommy into anything. He was a bright, intelligent young man, and capable of deciding what he wanted to do with his own life.

Clint had always been proud of his son, and there was a part of him now that was deeply concerned about Tommy's attitude toward Sierra. Why would he be so adamantly against her living on the ranch? Try as he might, Clint couldn't come up with a reason, unless...

Clint thoughtfully narrowed his eyes. Was Tommy thinking that his father's friendship with a woman was disloyal to his mother's memory? Clint thought about that idea for miles, considering it from many angles, and found it difficult to believe that was the problem. There were too many instances in the past where Tommy had teased him about women. Clint remembered one in particular. An attractive young woman who had worked in the small hardware store in Hillman for a few months had flirted with Clint every time he went in for something, and Tommy had thought it was pretty funny and had teased Clint unmercifully about it. "Ask her out, Dad. She'd say yes so fast your head would spin."

Clint hadn't asked her out. He'd simply had no interest in her as a woman. Truth was, he'd had no interest in any other woman since the day he'd met Janine.

He glanced at Sierra, felt her way down inside of himself, in the precise location that mattered to a man, and he suddenly needed more air. Inhaling deeply, he forced his eyes back to the road. He would not take advantage of Sierra's vulnerability, he told himself, he would not!

But things had gotten very complicated in the Barrow household, hadn't they?

Five

The Barrow Ranch was everything Clint had said it was, with a big old two-story house with a wraparound porch, miles of rolling green fields that gradually ascended into foothills, and uncountable herds of cattle and horses. A bonus to the valley's beauty was the distant snow-capped mountain range.

"It's wonderful, Clint," Sierra said as they got closer to the house.

"I've always thought so," he replied. "There's Rosie," he added, spotting her coming outside to meet them. His heart swelled when Tommy appeared, as well.

Clint parked in his usual spot and switched off the engine. Turning in his seat, he smiled at Sierra. "I'd like you to think of the ranch as home. I hope you can do that."

She took a moment, then smiled at him. "It's a lovely thought, Clint, and I'll certainly try. But I can't completely forget that I have a home of my own somewhere." Her smile faded as she said softly, "I must have."

It was an emotional moment, unexpected and dramatic, and Clint swallowed hard. It was strange how he felt Sierra's emotions so strongly. He couldn't remember having ever been so attuned to another person's feelings. When she smiled the sun seemed brighter, and when she didn't he felt her pain.

"Come and meet Rosie and Tommy," he said huskily. They got out of the pickup.

Rosie warmly welcomed Sierra. "There's a nice bedroom all ready and waiting for you."

"Thank you, Rosie." Sierra turned to Tommy. "Hello." He was a younger version of his father, tall and very handsome. "Thank you for saving my life, Tommy," she said.

Red spots appeared in his cheeks, and he looked at the ground. "I didn't do much," he mumbled.

Clint was so pleased that Tommy had made the effort to come outside and meet Sierra, and that last night's altercation was apparently forgotten, that he affectionately slapped his son on the back. "You did a great deal, son, and we all know it."

"Let's go in and get you settled," Rosie said to Sierra.

"Tommy and I'll bring in your things," Clint told her. "Go on in."

The two women walked away. Tommy frowned at his father. "What things, Dad?"

"I took Sierra shopping, Tommy. It's all in the back of the truck." When he opened the door of the canopy top, Tommy's mouth dropped open.

"What'd you do, buy out the mall?" he asked with a sarcastic twist of his lips.

Clint ignored the sarcasm. He was not going to have any more bitter words with Tommy if he could help it. Neither was he going to explain everything he did for Sierra, he thought as he began unloading sacks and bags. "Just about," he said cheerfully, as though Tommy, too, had spoken in that vein. "Grab an armful," he told his son, and started for the house.

Inside, Rosie was showing Sierra her room, which was on the first floor. The housekeeper was an energetic little woman with graying hair and a lively, friendly personality, and Sierra felt herself warming to her.

"My room is on this floor, too," Rosie said briskly. "Clint and Tommy sleep upstairs. Clint thought you'd do better on this floor because of the stairs, and look, this door opens onto the porch."

"It's a wonderful room, Rosie." Sierra liked the high ceilings of the house, the ornate woodwork. The bedroom furniture gleamed with polish, and the matching fabric of the bedspread and curtains was hunter green with tiny white flowers.

Clint arrived with his load and deposited it on the bed. "Goodness," Rosie exclaimed. "What's this?"

"Sierra's clothes." He smiled at Sierra and left for another load.

Rosie had not missed the smile, nor Sierra's quick response to it. She said nothing about it, of course, though the idea of Clint at long last having a woman friend warmed her sixty-year-old heart. "There are a few hangers in the closet, but it looks to me like you're going to need more than what's in there. I'll go get some." Rosie hurried out.

Sierra used the moment alone to step out onto the porch. Clint was right. It was peaceful here. Quiet and peaceful! A beautiful valley, a special place. Would her memory return quicker in this place of serenity and scenic splendor than in town?

Tommy came in, saw where Clint had put the packages he'd carried in, and dropped his on the bed, also. He saw Sierra on the porch through the open door. She seemed to be deep in her own thoughts, and he turned and left quickly so she wouldn't spot him and want to talk.

Finally everything had been brought in. The bed was

overflowing, even though the things that had been left on
hangers by thoughtful salesclerks were already in the closet.
Clint and Tommy had left Sierra alone, and the job of putting all those new clothes away suddenly seemed overwhelming. She sank into a chair, feeling achy again and
tired, very tired. She put her head back, thinking that she
would rest for a few minutes before tackling all those packages.

Rosie came in with hangers and scissors. "I'm going to
clear the bed for you," she announced in her get-things-
done way. "Just sit right where you are. I'll have everything put away in no time."

The last thing Sierra intended doing while she was in
this house was to impose on Rosie's—or anyone else's—
time. "I can do it, Rosie, really. I was just…resting a moment."

"Of course you were resting. Why wouldn't you need
rest? Goodness, you just got out of the hospital, and then
all that shopping. Well, you're not to move from that chair,
hear?" She began opening sacks and taking out clothes.

Sierra sat still and watched Rosie snip away prices tags
and fill bureau drawers and the closet. Rosie's comments,
"My, this is pretty," or "This color is perfect for you,"
all ran together while Sierra's mind worked and strained.

*I can read and write: I haven't forgotten the essentials.
Just who I am, or was; what I did; where I lived; my family,
if I have one; my own life; the personal stuff that made me
an individual. Am I the same person I was before the accident, only without a memory? Did my personality
change? Was I kind, like Clint? Like Rosie?*

"Sierra? I'm all done, Sierra. Why don't you change into
one of those pretty nightgowns and get into bed? You'll
get a crick in your neck sleeping in that chair."

I wasn't sleeping, but I would like to, for days. Even
with sedatives she hadn't slept well in the hospital. Pray
God she wouldn't have that problem here.

"Thank you, Rosie."

"Supper's at six, Sierra. But if you sleep through the supper hour and want something to eat later on, either help yourself or knock on my door. It's the one at the very end of the hall. The bathroom on this floor is right next door. Honey, would you like some help getting undressed?"

Sierra pulled herself to her feet. "Thank you, Rosie, but I can manage. And thank you for putting everything away."

"You look and sound exhausted." Rosie walked to the door. "Go to bed and don't get up until you feel like it. If that's not until tomorrow, so be it."

"I'll be fine, Rosie. Thank you for your concern."

"Well, don't hesitate to ask for anything you might need." Rosie left, closing the door behind her.

Sierra found her nightclothes in the second drawer of the dresser. She took out a nightgown, undressed and slipped the gown over her head. Then she drew back the covers and crawled into bed.

She fell into a deep sleep in minutes.

Clint was worried about Sierra not showing up for supper, but when Rosie told him that she'd been worn-out and had gone to bed, he tried to settle his nerves and enjoy Rosie's fine meal.

Two ranch hands ate with the family. Clint employed four other men, but with the ranch being so large—six thousand acres—there were stations scattered across it, where they lived. Those four hands rarely appeared at the main compound. Clint went to them, in his pickup or on horseback, or talked to them by telephone.

The two men living in the compound stayed in the bunkhouse, which was located some distance from the house with the other buildings—the barns, equipment and storage sheds, the corrals and feeding pens. When Clint's great-grandfather had constructed the present house, he had deliberately built it a good distance from the animals and outbuildings, as his wife, Clint's great-grandmother, had had an aversion to the smells that were part and parcel of raising cattle and horses.

Thus, the house was somewhat isolated from the business end of the ranch. It was surrounded by acres of lawn and massive old trees, and Rosie, being a natural-born gardener, had put in flower beds years ago. Every spring she planted a vegetable garden as well, and though the growing season was short in this high country, she was delighted when the green onions matured, or the lettuce, the radishes. Carrots, potatoes, beans, peas, tomatoes and corn matured later, and sometimes an early frost would kill the plants, but she never let one year's defeat destroy her enthusiasm for the following year's crop.

Clint liked Rosie's garden. Not because of the food it produced, but because watching things grow was a comforting pastime. Almost every evening he walked in the garden and inspected the plants.

He did so after supper, but found himself glancing toward the house more than checking the progress of the onion sets. He was so aware of Sierra's presence on the ranch that he could think of little else. She was here, under his roof, and he thought of how much he liked her, and of how much he would like her to remain in his house.

Which she wouldn't do after her memory returned. Dare he wish that she never did recover her past? That he would even think such a thing was startling. And alarming. How could she ever be truly happy, not knowing who she was? And he wanted her to be happy, didn't he?

Disturbed by the ramblings of his mind, he left the garden and hiked down to the barns. The compound was quiet. Tommy had gone somewhere right after supper, and Clint knew Rosie's habits: she would be in her room now, watching TV.

Clint rarely watched television. Usually he retired shortly after dark and read in bed until he got sleepy. Tonight he didn't feel like reading *or* going to bed, and knew exactly why he felt so restless: Sierra.

Leaning against a corral fence, he could see the back of the house and the lighted windows of Rosie's room. The kitchen lights were on, too. Turning his head a little, he could see the bunkhouse lights. Everything was normal.

Everything but him. In the pit of his stomach was a churning sensation. Sierra...Sierra. Her name repeated in his mind. It was ironic that if she was still in the hospital he would be sitting with her, talking to her, looking at her, and here on the ranch he wasn't seeing her at all.

As it got darker the automatic yard lights came on. The sudden infusion of light seemed to intrude on his privacy, and he moved away from the corral and slowly walked back to the house.

But instead of going in, he rounded the house and climbed the front porch stairs to sit in the dark and think, to question and ponder fate. A seemingly unnecessary collision, Sierra being on that treacherous road, Tommy running late that morning and taking the shortcut over Cougar Pass. It had changed Clint's life, hadn't it? Changed his outlook, too. He no longer felt contented. Anxiety was what he felt now, and restless, sexual stirrings, yearnings of the heart and mind. Sierra...Sierra...

Inside the house, Sierra awoke with a start. She sat up. Someone had been calling her name. It didn't seem like a dream, and she listened hard for a few moments. Sighing, she lay down again. It had to have been a dream. She was still tired and would soon go back to sleep.

But the room suddenly seemed airless. She didn't want a light on—the darkness felt good—but she needed some fresh air. Sliding out of bed, she went to the door leading to the front porch and opened it. The cool night air felt wonderful on her skin, and she took long, full breaths of it, drawing it deeply into her lungs.

Clint nearly choked when that door opened. Turning his

head, he saw her. She was standing in the doorway, neither in the bedroom or on the porch. There was enough starlight for him to make out her form and the paleness of a long gown. Her hair wasn't nipped at her nape, as it usually was, but cascaded over her shoulders and bosom. She didn't know he was there, he realized.

While he watched, she raised her hands to lift her hair from the back of her neck, as though needing to cool her skin. His pulse began racing; he'd never seen anything more sensuous in his life.

But he felt like an intruder. She thought she was alone, and she should know that she wasn't.

"Sierra?" he said softly, getting up from the chair.

She recognized his voice at once and didn't jump or start. "Clint," she said, almost drowsily. The fresh air was reviving and certainly smelled marvelous, but she still felt languorous, her eyes heavy-lidded from sleeping so hard, and she let her hair drop slowly. "What time is it?"

"Around nine."

"I slept a long time."

He was staring, trying to see her better in such feeble light, still only able to make out her form, the way her face, arms and gown all seemed to be one pale blur in contrast to her mass of dark hair. "Obviously you needed the sleep," he said, not thinking of time at all, nor of sleep. How could those topics compete with her, with the way he felt about her?

There, he'd acknowledged his feelings openly and honestly, if only to himself. He could so easily fall in love with her, or maybe he already had.

Sierra took another deep breath, then stepped onto the porch and went to the railing. The cold wood floor felt good on the bottom of her bare feet, as did the cool night air on her face and arms. She'd been too warm in bed and should have opened a window before going to sleep. Tomorrow she would investigate how the windows in her room opened so she wouldn't have the same problem again.

Clint was mesmerized. He could not have imagined Sierra coming outside like this, but then his imagination hadn't been stretched in this direction for a good many years.

He couldn't stop himself. He quietly walked up behind her and put his hands on the railing on each side of her. He heard the breath she sucked in and knew he had startled her.

But she didn't tell him to move. In fact, she crossed her own arms over her breasts and leaned back against him. His heart began pounding. He dipped his head to bury his face in her hair. The scent of her filled his nostrils, his brain, and sent his senses flying.

"Sierra," he whispered. The sensation of her body against his, the silkiness of her gown, the realization of how flimsy a garment it really was, had his head spinning. Nothing could affect him as strongly as her acquiescence, however. It seemed utterly astounding to him that she was permitting this to happen. Astounding and wonderful. He let go of the railing and crossed his arms over hers, bringing her closer, holding her tighter.

Sierra felt as though her heart had risen to her throat. She could feel its hard, erratic beat there. Clint's warmth was saturating her system, and it was a heavenly, delicious sensation. Oh, the joy of feeling like this, she thought dreamily, the wonder of it.

She suddenly wanted Clint's kiss on her lips, and she turned in his arms. Her breasts were against his chest, her thighs against his. She tipped her head back to see his face, and it was only a second before he kissed her.

Moaning softly, she snuggled closer and slid her arms up around his neck. She felt at home in his arms, as though they had held each other like this many times. There was passion underlying the gentleness of his mouth on hers, and she felt her own system catch fire. His tongue slipped between her lips, and her excitement multiplied tenfold. She strained against him, wanting all of him.

Clint was dizzy with desire. She was kissing him with abandon, with unmistakable hunger. It didn't surprise him. They had bonded at their very first meeting, and he'd known from that moment that there was something special and wonderful between them. It was bound to take this direction.

"Sierra," he whispered thickly in a brief moment between kisses that were no longer gentle. He slid his hands down the silky fabric of her gown to caress and cup her buttocks, to draw her closer to the almost agonizing center of his need.

He's so aroused, but so am I. Have I ever wanted a man more?

It was a deadly question, reminding Sierra of her amnesia. She might be married. More, she might be in love with her husband. Tears sprang to her eyes, and she jerked free of Clint's embrace. "We—we can't do this," she whispered hoarsely.

He didn't have to ask her why they couldn't; he knew exactly what she was thinking. His hands dangled at his sides, clenching and unclenching.

"I'm sorry," he said, his voice conveying total misery. "I shouldn't have touched you, but you're so beautiful and I've felt something special for you from the first. Sierra, there's been no one since..." he couldn't bring himself to mention Janine's name "...for five years now. It's important to me that you know that."

She wiped her eyes and tried to get hold of herself. Still, when she spoke, her voice sounded ragged. "I believe you, Clint."

"I didn't invite you here to take advantage of you."

"I know." She didn't deny having special feelings for him; she couldn't. But it was the woman she was now who was falling in love with Clint, and if a husband or lover should suddenly come to light…?

She shuddered as the enormity of her situation hit her with devastating force.

"You're getting cold," Clint said. "It's time you went back inside, Sierra." He put his arm around her shoulders, and for just a moment Sierra laid her head on his chest, then lifted it and let him lead her to the door of her room.

"Good night," she whispered huskily before going in.

"Good night. Sleep well."

After the door closed behind her, Clint walked to the railing, clasping it so tightly his knuckles ached. As he studied the stars he felt as though his heart was breaking. He wanted Sierra to get well; he could never *really* wish for anything else.

But when she did, everything would change. She would leave the ranch, leave him and return to…to what? There had to be someone waiting for her to come home, probably wondering by now why she *wasn't* home.

Clint sighed deeply, heavily. One question played and replayed in his mind. When the day came that she knew who she was again and returned to her former life, how would he go on without her?

The future loomed dark and lonely. Without Sierra in it, that's how it looked to Clint.

Six

With her heart knocking against her rib cage, Sierra listened at the door until she heard Clint leaving the porch. Actually, she couldn't tell if he'd left the porch or merely walked around it, but he was no longer near the door to her bedroom.

She climbed into bed then and pulled the blankets up to her chin, her eyes wide and staring. All she could think of was Clint and how much she had wanted his kisses to go on and on. The throbbing aches in her body now had nothing at all to do with the accident. There was a deep yearning in the pit of her stomach that seemed to affect even her skin, and it caused a discomfiting restlessness of spirit that had her biting her lips and heaving tremendous, emotion-laden sighs.

If only I could remember. Desperately seeking something from her past, Sierra slid her hands from beneath the covers and pressed her fingertips to her temples. Gently she massaged, as though the circular movement would send electrical impulses to her brain and relax it enough to release its tight grip on her memory. If there was no man, no husband, waiting and worrying about her, she would unleash her feelings for Clint, but how could she let herself behave as she'd done tonight when she might be a married woman with children?

All she attained from her concentrated efforts was a headache. Dr. Trugood had told her that she would not be able to force memory, and that her best course was to relax and let it happen. How could she relax, for heaven's sake? How could she forget that her life, as she knew it, began less than two weeks ago? Dr. Trugood had also told her that if she wished to talk to him after she left the hospital, he would be happy to see her in his office.

Would it help? Sierra wondered. She would do almost anything to penetrate the shell encasing her memory, and she felt certain that Clint would drive her to Missoula for appointments with the psychologist.

She sighed again heavily, despondently, and moved restlessly, trying to find a comfortable position. Truth was, she didn't know what she should do. If she *could* relax, if she could stop her incessant attempts to remember, maybe it *would* happen on its own.

"Oh, Clint," she whispered, once again lost in the magical moments between them on the porch. Was she a naturally passionate woman, or was her response to Clint something special?

She squeezed her eyes shut in a torrent of emotional pain. Only seconds after promising herself to stop trying so hard to remember, she was doing it again. Tears began seeping from her eyes. She felt helpless and hopeless, and there was nothing she could do about it, nothing.

A thought suddenly struck her with thundering impact. She should have let Clint take her to the accident site today! She had to see it, however frightening the prospect. But it was where her old life had ended and her new one began, and if that didn't jolt her senses and stir her memory, would anything?

"Clint, I made a mistake yesterday," Sierra said, obviously uncomfortable with the admission.

Clint thought she was referring to what had happened on the porch last night. They were seated at the dining table, and Sierra wouldn't quite meet his eyes. He had eaten breakfast with the men several hours ago, but had joined Sierra for a cup of coffee when he'd spotted her eating alone.

He took a disheartened breath. "I'm sorry about that, Sierra. All I can tell you is that it won't happen again."

For a moment she lifted her gaze and looked blank. Then she realized what he'd meant. "It's not that, Clint," she said quietly, dropping her eyes again. "Maybe that, too, was a mistake, but it's not the one I was talking about."

The dining room was bright with morning sunlight, highlighting Sierra's glossy dark hair. Even with partially healed abrasions on her face, Clint thought she was the most beautiful woman he'd ever seen. Her heavily lashed eyes were slightly almond shaped and tilted up at their outer corners. He couldn't look at her lovely mouth without thinking of kissing it again.

Still, he tried. "Tell me what's bothering you," he said gently.

She stared down at the table for a moment, then forced herself to look directly at him. "I should have let you take me to the accident site yesterday. I thought about it last night after—after…" She dropped that subject and continued. "Would you mind driving me there today? I hate asking, Clint. I promised myself before ever leaving the hospital that I would not get in the way of your daily routines. But this seems so crucial. I wish I had realized that yesterday."

"The idea frightened you yesterday. Are you sure you're ready to go there?"

Nervously Sierra took a sip of coffee and set her cup down. "To be honest, I'm not sure of anything. Dr. Trugood said to relax. I—I can't do it. If there's the remotest chance something at that site will trigger my memory, I have to try."

Clint set down his own cup and reached for her hand. Not only did she let him take it, she wound her fingers through his. Clint gave her hope, strength and a sense of security. He had from the beginning. There was something very powerful between them, and while they both knew it couldn't go anywhere until she recovered her past, neither of them could deny its presence and influence.

"I'll take you anywhere you want to go," he said softly. "I'll do anything I can to help. You must believe that, Sierra." His feelings for her shone in his eyes and Sierra saw them, felt them in her soul.

"Thank you," she whispered.

Clint's chest constricted. He felt a rush of emotion stronger than anything he'd ever known before. But he didn't dare say so. He had no right. She could be another man's wife, and when she regained her memory she would also remember her love for that man.

He cleared his throat. "Would you like to go this morning?"

"Can you take the time this morning?" She hoped he didn't feel the sudden fear in her system through his grasp on her hand.

"I can do anything I want." He attempted a smile, which turned out to be feeble but sincere. "Remember, I own this ranch." Giving her hand a squeeze, he let go of it. "I'll drive you there right now, if you'd like."

Better to get it over with, she thought with an inner shudder. Why the idea of visiting the accident site should bother

her so much was a mystery, but maybe it was a mystery
that would unravel itself once she saw the place.

"Yes," she said, pushing back her chair. "If you can go
now, let's do it."

Nodding, Clint got to his feet. She was a woman with
immense courage, because he sensed how much she *didn't*
want to do this.

Well, neither did he. He had a strong, painful premoni-
tion that the day she remembered her past would be the
day he'd lose her. If it happened today, so soon, would he
be able to bear it?

His expression was grim as they left the dining room and
then the house to go to his pickup. But when he opened
the passenger door for Sierra to get in, he gave her a smile
that was entirely for her benefit.

He sure as hell didn't feel like smiling for his own.

Sierra saw almost at once that Clint was driving an entirely different route than the one he'd taken from Missoula.
He made several turns this morning and the roads were
mostly gravel, whereas they had been on asphalt all the
way from Missoula.

She tried to quell the nervous fluttering in her stomach—
not from the roads, but because of what she might discover
at the accident site. Rather, what she might *not* discover. If
nothing happened, if she remembered nothing at all, she
would be sorely disappointed.

Clint could tell how tight she felt. Her right hand clasped
the armrest as though letting go of it would send her flying
out of the truck. Her left was curled into a fist on her lap.
Sensing what she was going through, or at least suspecting
it, he tried to ease her tension with simple conversation.

"These back roads are usable only during good
weather," he said calmly. "During the winter months,
they're usually snowed in, and since no one lives on them,
the county doesn't plow them." He swerved to avoid a

pothole. "They're not kept in top-notch condition, as you can tell, although repairs are made by county crews periodically."

Sierra knew that he was trying to get her mind off their destination, truly appreciated his effort and forced herself to answer. "If no one lives out here, why are there roads at all?"

"There were a lot of logging and mining operations in the area some years back. These roads are leftovers, I guess you might call them. They're not shown on state maps and only the locals use them." He amended that statement. "Locals and people deliberately looking for little-used back roads."

"Explorers," Sierra murmured. Was that what she'd been doing that fateful day—exploring back roads? Clint turned onto another road, and suddenly the mountains were just ahead. The route became steeper as it began winding upward.

He sent her a concerned glance. If this narrow mountain road frightened her, he would turn back. "How are you doing?" he asked, trying desperately to sound normal.

"I'm all right. The mountains are beautiful."

The awe in her voice surprised him. Puzzled him, as well. He'd thought that her tension would increase in a direct ratio with the elevation. Apparently it wasn't. He'd driven this road countless times, and there was no question that the scenery was spectacular, but he had not expected Sierra to appreciate the views.

It was time she knew exactly where she was. He spoke quietly. "This is the road to Cougar Pass. It's the one Tommy and Eric were on that morning."

Sierra's breath caught for a moment, then she managed a shaky response. "And the one I was on, also. Coming from the other direction."

"Yes." The road was treacherous and he had to keep his eyes on it, but he stole a quick glance at Sierra. A fraction of a second was all it took to see that she was no longer awestruck by the scenery. She was so tense, in fact, that she was straining against the seat belt to sit on the edge of the seat.

He'd been driving very slowly, which was how he always drove this road. It was how anyone with any sense at all drove it. He wasn't thinking of that, however; his thoughts were on Sierra, and he couldn't bear her agony one minute more. The next curve was a good quarter of a mile ahead, so this was a safe enough place to stop, and he put on the brakes.

Unfastening his own safety belt, he slid across the seat and put his arms around Sierra. "You don't have to do this," he told her, his voice breaking with emotion.

She let him hold her, even laid her head on his chest. The moment was a respite from the fear she'd been enduring, one she desperately needed. Besides, being in Clint's arms warmed her heart and body as nothing else in her life—as she knew it these days—could do. Every time Clint touched her it felt as though he was transferring some part of himself to her, passing strength and willpower from his system to hers.

But there was more than those things keeping her in his arms. He was an incredible, wonderful man, and she realized that she wanted to *know* him as a man. She couldn't help feeling as she did about him; she couldn't destroy the desire he aroused within her. His kisses last night had spoken volumes, telling Sierra he wanted her. Did wanting him in the same way make her an immoral woman? At this moment, did she care?

She slid her hand down his chest and laid it high on his thigh, a provocative advance. Clint's pulse went wild. He knew he should stop her, but his body had ceased taking orders from his brain.

"Do you mind?" she whispered. "I...I need to touch you."

His voice was ragged and hoarse. "Do anything you want." Last night on the porch she had kissed him back, passionately, and he would have done to her what she was doing to him today if she hadn't decided against further intimacy. How far would she go? his befuddled mind wondered. He was afraid to take the initiative for fear of squelching her curiosity. Was it possible she couldn't remember what a man's body was like?

In the next heartbeat he quit worrying about initiative or anything else, because he could not resist kissing her. Holding the back of her head in his right hand, he tilted her chin with his left and pressed his mouth to hers. Almost instantly he felt crazed with desire. But it was broad daylight, and while this road wasn't used very much, a car could come along. He tried very hard to remember that fact while his tongue plunged into her mouth and she grew bolder in exploring the front of his jeans, but it quickly lost import as his blood pressure approached an explosive high.

Sierra suddenly felt restrained by her seat belt and flicked open the latch to give them more freedom of movement. In that instant something flashed through her mind. *She had opened her seat belt during the accident!*

She began struggling, tearing her mouth from Clint's. "Clint...I remember something!"

Dazed, he stared at her, trying desperately to focus his eyes on her glowing face. His body was on fire, and for several moments he could think of nothing else, but finally he grasped what she'd said and took a long, shaky breath to clear his head.

"What—what do you remember?" His voice sounded like a rusty hinge, but he was trying.

"I unlatched my seat belt during the accident! I remember doing it." Sierra's excitement began fading. "It's not much to go on, is it?"

Clint was still attempting to cool down. "It's a start.

Let's talk about it a little. Do you remember being frightened? Did you realize what you were doing, and why?''

"I...don't know. When I opened my seat belt just now, I got this picture, clear as a bell. But it's gone now. It's gone.'' She turned to look at him, then nestled against his chest again. "I'm so frightened, Clint,'' she whispered.

He heaved a long, wistful sigh. He could probably arouse her again, but this was no place to be making love. It was best that *something* had happened to stop them, however much his aching body preferred otherwise.

Tenderly he brushed straying strands of hair from her face. "Do you still want to see the accident site?''

She shuddered. "No, I wish I never had to see it. But I have to go there, Clint, I—I have to.''

"Whatever you say.'' He took her face in his hands and whispered, "I want to make love to you. You know that, don't you?''

"Yes, I know it, and I want...I want...'' Biting her lip, she stopped herself. "It doesn't matter what we want. I could be married.''

"You could also be single.''

"If I am, why do I have this indentation on my ring finger?''.

"Sierra, not all rings are wedding rings.''

"You're right, of course, but until I know for sure...'' Sierra moved over and fastened her seat belt. "Please, let's just go.''

She sounded weary and discouraged. Clint's heart went out to her, but he didn't reach for her again, not even to offer comfort. He knew that a simple hug was impossible for them now. It would explode into passion, just as it had last night and today. With a grim set to his lips, he slid across the seat and hooked his own seat belt.

He had just put the truck in motion when Sierra said in the saddest voice he'd ever heard, "Maybe I'll never know for sure.'' Her eyes, pleading and haunted, turned to him.

"Oh, Clint, what if I don't? What if I never regain my memory?"

He swallowed hard. "Don't think about that, honey. You'll remember everything one of these days. You just need more time."

Her gaze remained on him. "You're a prince among men, Clint."

He took his eyes from the road long enough to send her a little half smile. "Thanks, but I'm as ordinary as they come."

"No, Clint, you're not." Holding back tears, she faced front and stared out the windshield.

Clint himself felt tense as they got nearer to the hairpin curve where the accident had taken place. He was worried how Sierra would react. She might remember everything, she might remember nothing. Neither option was comforting.

When he finally saw the curve up ahead, he also saw a line of orange cones on the roadway, and some signs.

"We're nearly there," he said, speaking as calmly as he could.

Sierra had been noticing something about herself—she loved colors. It was a personal trait, she felt, and had nothing to do with memory. But everything had a color, and she liked comparing soft, powdery hues with bright, bold shades. The orange cones in the road ahead were eye-catching, and obviously out of sync with the green mountains and dun-colored road.

As they got closer to the signs Clint read aloud, 'Caution. Road Repairs Ahead.' I doubt that anyone's working on the road, but someone's doing something around that curve."

Sierra's heart skipped a beat. "The accident investigators John Mann told me about?"

"Probably," Clint agreed, and glanced at her with a concerned frown. "Are you all right?"

She forced herself to sit up straighter. She had to do this, and she had whined about it quite enough. "I'm fine."

Clint slowed down to a crawl. The sharp curve bent back upon itself, the worst segment of the Cougar Pass road. On their right was a high, rocky bluff, and there was nothing on the left side of the road at all, just that sheer drop to the river. Rounding the curve, he immediately saw more orange cones and three vehicles parked and hugging the bluff. He pulled to a stop behind a Montana Highway Patrol car, turned off the ignition and looked at Sierra, who was frowning and biting her lower lip.

"This is it?" she asked anxiously. "This is the place?"

"This is it," he said quietly. Her eyes seemed to be darting around, and he didn't have to ask if anything was familiar because the answer was written all over her face: nothing was.

She spoke dully. "What in God's name was I doing out here?" She didn't expect Clint to answer that question. In fact, she had asked it of herself, not of him. "You told me once that this road leads to Cougar Mountain. Did we pass it?"

"No. We can go back that way, if you'd like, but I turned onto this road about twenty miles this side of the mountain." He reached out and took her hand, and, as always, she let him hold it. "Do you want to get out and look around?"

She nodded. "Since I don't intend to come back here, yes, I think I should." She turned her head to see his face, and the caring, concerned expression in his wonderful blue eyes made her heart skip. She could break down very easily right now, she knew, and she didn't want to do any more crying on Clint's shoulder today. He was so patient with her, so considerate of her moods, and perhaps he always would be. But he didn't deserve to have an almost constantly emotional woman on his hands. She spoke with a firmness she certainly didn't feel, "I want to see it all. I'm ready when you are."

Clint knew what she was doing—burying her emotions for his sake. Her consideration touched him, as everything about her did. She shouldn't have to do this, he thought unhappily. She shouldn't have to dig and delve into a forgotten past. She was a special person just as she was, and if she could accept that...

But she couldn't, of course. He wouldn't be able to if it were him with amnesia.

"I'm ready," he said a bit gruffly. "Get out my side. We're too close to the bluff for your door to open." When she slid over, he helped her out of the truck.

No one was in sight, but they could hear voices mingled with the sound of rushing water. The drivers of the parked cars had to be down by the river.

Clint took Sierra's hand and walked her across the road to the edge of the ravine. Looking down, she gasped out loud, and he protectively laid his arm around her shoulders. He realized that no one had explained the particulars of the accident to her when she said in a whispery, shaky voice, "Tell me exactly what happened."

Watching the men working at the river's edge, obviously combing the area for wreckage, Clint recited the details, keeping his voice even and unemotional. Sierra tried to visualize his words, to picture her van tumbling end over end to the river's edge, to see herself being thrown out on the rocks, to *remember!*

The images in her mind were horrifying, but they were from her imagination, not memory. There was nothing for her here. Forcing herself to come and see the accident site had done no good at all.

Discouraged and sick at heart, she said unsteadily, "I'd like to go now. May we?"

"Yes," Clint murmured, feeling a little sick at heart himself.

The men below had spotted them, and one of them called, "Hello up there! Something we can do for you?"

Clint called back, "This is the lady who was driving the van. She wanted to see where the accident happened. We're leaving now."

With his arm still around her shoulders, he brought Sierra back to his truck. She had no idea how he got the vehicle turned around, because she felt so totally numb she wasn't registering anything. All she could think of was that deep rocky slope and the rushing river. How had she lived through such a horrible accident?

No wonder the doctors at the hospital had marveled over her trivial injuries. Her *physical* injuries, that is.

Seven

That evening Clint caught his son just as he was going out the back door. "Tommy, I need to talk to you. Could you come to the office, please?"

"Dad, I'm picking up Eric. We're going to a party in town and I'm already late. How about doing our talking tomorrow?"

Clint weighed the matter. Tommy was freshly shaved and showered. His dark hair was still damp, and he had on clean clothes. Excitement shone in his eyes. All week Tommy had participated in pregraduation activities. Tomorrow night's ceremony would put an end to his high school years. His eighteenth birthday was only a month away. He hadn't been a child for a long time, but in Clint's eyes, neither was he a man.

"This won't take long, Tom, just a few minutes. Come along." Clint walked away, heading for the office, aware of Tommy following behind him, albeit grudgingly.

Clint closed the office door and sat behind the desk.

Tommy stood by, looking anxious to be off. Ignoring his son's air of impatience, Clint said firmly, "I'd like you to tell me what's bothering you. I know it has to do with Sierra being here, but there has to be a reason why her staying with us annoys you."

Tommy shifted from one foot to the other and looked everywhere but into his father's eyes. "Uh, you're wrong, Dad." He shrugged nonchalantly. "Why would I care if she's here?"

"I'm not wrong, and why you would care is precisely my question. Tommy, you were rude to her during dinner. You hardly said two words."

"Neither did she."

"True, but she has a lot on her mind."

"From what I've heard, she doesn't have *anything* on her mind."

Clint winced. "That's a cruel thing to say, Tommy. She's an intelligent woman with a memory loss. Exactly what is it about her that puts you off so much?"

Tommy's face reddened. "She doesn't belong here," he blurted.

"Out of sight, out of mind? Tommy, wherever Sierra might be living, she is always going to be the driver of that van. I know you're not over the accident, and maybe I'd be the same. Maybe anyone would. But, son, you saved her life. You should be bursting-your-buttons proud of what you did. Instead—and I'll be damned if I can figure out why—you resent my helping Sierra through what has to be a very bad time for her."

Tommy stared at the floor for a long moment, then mumbled, "You like her. I don't mean just 'cause you think you should be helping her. You really like her, I can tell."

"And that's why you *don't* like her? Tommy, look at me, please." Clint was stunned by the belligerence in his son's eyes when he finally raised them. "You don't just resent Sierra, you resent me. That's quite a blow, son."

"I don't resent anyone," Tommy said defiantly. "Can I go now?"

Clint felt utterly defeated. For the first time ever he couldn't get through to his son. There were things going on in Tommy's head he couldn't or wouldn't talk about, and that had never happened before. Clint honestly didn't know how to deal with it.

"Yes," he said quietly. "You can go now."

Tommy left so fast he was a blur. Clint stared at the empty doorway, feeling a little heartsick. The last thing he would ever want was a break with his son, and it was happening and he didn't know what to do about it.

No, maybe he did know what would change everything: moving Sierra back to Missoula.

But that was something he couldn't do. Not even for Tommy.

Sierra wandered into the kitchen the following afternoon, where Rosie was busy preparing a special dinner to celebrate Tommy's graduation. "Is there anything I can do to help?" she asked.

Rosie looked pleased at the offer. "How about frosting that sheet cake on the counter? It's chocolate, Tommy's favorite, and the icing is all made. Just needs to be put on the cake, and I'd like it spread smoothly so I can decorate it with a few words of congratulations."

"Yes, I think I can manage to do that." Rosie was a good cook, and Sierra wondered about herself. Was she capable of putting a decent meal on the table or was she all thumbs in a kitchen? Well, anyone could spread icing on a cake, she told herself with an inner sigh. Rosie handed her a wide knife and Sierra began the process.

The white icing flowed smoothly over the dark cake, and Sierra found herself fascinated with the contrasting colors. But then the cake was completely covered and she stared at the rectangle of white, again feeling a twinge of memory that had to do with the color. Or lack thereof, she reminded herself. What was there about colors that teased and taunted her so?

"It's done," she said to Rosie.

Rosie looked at the frosted cake. "Oh, it's pretty, smooth as glass."

"What do you want written on it, Rosie?"

"Would you like to decorate it?" Rosie went to a cupboard for a small box that Sierra saw contained four tiny vials of food coloring—red, green, blue and yellow.

"Yes, I think I would." Sierra frowned. "But what if I ruin it?"

"Hon, you don't need to be an artist to decorate a cake with a few words. Here's the extra icing. Divide it into smaller bowls, add the coloring, mix it up and squirt it through this here gadget." Rosie produced a soft pouch with a metal tip. "You just put the icing in this pouch and squeeze it through the end. It works real well."

What interested Sierra most about Rosie's instructions was the part about adding colors to the icing. She spooned some of the white icing into a small bowl and gingerly added one drop of red coloring. Stirring the mixture, she found the icing turned a pretty pale pink. A second drop of coloring deepened the pink, and a third produced a rosy hue.

Excitement coursed through Sierra's veins. She took out more small bowls and made blue icing, green icing, yellow icing. Then she combined the red and blue dyes and produced lavender icing, and then orange icing by using the red and yellow dyes.

"Well, for goodness sakes," Rosie exclaimed, eyeing the orange and lavender bowls. "How'd you do that?"

"We have the primary colors here, Rosie—red, yellow and blue. Red and yellow make orange, yellow and blue make green and red and blue make purple. Those are called binary colors. Along with white and black, you can produce every color known to mankind with primary colors.''

"Is that a fact? Well, you have white," Rosie noted.

"But not black, which is necessary to produce deep or dark shades.''

"You have got to be an artist to know so much about colors," Rosie declared.

Sierra laughed. "Or a house painter." Rosie laughed, too, and left Sierra to her cake decorating. But Sierra had discovered something important about herself, and it felt like a momentous stride forward.

Her decorated cake turned out so startlingly beautiful that Rosie couldn't praise it enough.

It seemed, Sierra thought happily, that she *was* an artist. She proved it again later by doing some pencil sketching, surprising herself at how accurately she could draw a tree, a horse or a scene of the ranch house.

But there was no color in her sketches, and she yearned for it, for some kind of paints or pastels. She said nothing about it to anyone because she didn't have the money to buy art supplies, and she would not ask Clint to buy them for her.

He had already spent far too much money on her.

Although both Rosie and Clint invited Sierra to attend Tommy's graduation ceremony with them that evening, she refused with thanks. She simply wasn't ready to face a large gathering and could see no sensible reason to force herself to do so.

Clint felt differently. He hated leaving her home alone, and getting her out and away from the ranch, whatever the function, made sense to him. Tommy had left for town earlier, so it was just Clint and Rosie in his truck when he asked, "How do *you* think Sierra is doing, Rosie?"

"Well, she's a quiet little thing," Rosie replied after thinking about it a moment. "Pleasant woman, though, and

you saw what she did with Tommy's cake. She's an artist,
Clint. I'd swear an oath on it.''

"The cake was special, all right."

"You should hear her talk about colors, and mixing them
to make different ones. Oh, yes, she's definitely been involved in some sort of art. I saw her outside with a pad
and pencil this afternoon, and it looked to me like she was
drawing pictures. She didn't show me what she'd been doing, so I can't say for sure, of course, but that's the im-
pression I got.''

"Interesting," Clint murmured. If Sierra had discovered
a talent for drawing or whatever, why hadn't she mentioned
it to him? It could, after all, be a breakthrough to her past,
perhaps the first link of a chain that would gradually
lengthen until she remembered everything.

At once the mixed emotions he always felt when he
thought of Sierra fully recovered gripped him. He wanted
her well, but at the same time he didn't want to lose her.
He suspected strongly that when she remembered her former life she would return to it. Wouldn't anyone? If the
same thing happened to him, for instance—if he was driving in an unfamiliar area and an accident caused him to
lose his memory—the day he remembered the ranch and
Tommy he would head home. It was only natural to assume
Sierra would react similarly.

And yet he couldn't wish or hope for a permanent memory loss for Sierra. That would be unforgivably selfish, and
he had never been selfish or self-centered in all of his life.
It was an uncomfortable dilemma to be dealing with—
wanting her well, wanting her in his life and knowing the
two desires might never come to fruition.

He sighed quietly, keeping his eyes on the road, only
partially aware of Rosie talking about the evening ahead.
This was an important night for Tommy—for himself, as
well—and Rosie was more excited about it than he was.

Feeling guilty about that, Clint tried to put Sierra out of his mind and gear up his own excitement.

"Tommy's all set for his trip," he said.

"Oh my, yes," Rosie agreed with a laugh. "He's been packed for days. Goodness, the ranch won't be the same with Tommy gone for two weeks."

"No, it won't be the same," Clint said quietly. Months ago he had promised Tommy a two-week vacation in southern California for a graduation present. Eric's parents had done the same for their son. Tommy was going to stay with the Schulzes tonight, and the boys would be up early tomorrow morning to catch their flight to Los Angeles. They had reserved a beachfront condo. Their plans included seeing the sights and spending long lazy days on the beach. Clint had not been the least bit concerned about the two boys' adventure so far from home, but with Tommy acting so strange and withdrawn since the accident, he wasn't as comfortable with the idea as he'd once been.

But perhaps the only thing happening with Tommy was that he was growing up, Clint told himself—growing up and away from his father. It was bound to happen sooner or later, wasn't it? Kids eventually cut the apron strings in a perfectly natural biological urge to be on their own. It was just that Clint had never thought it would happen with him and Tommy. Tommy had always come to him about everything. They'd talked repeatedly about girls, sex, politics, religion and any other topic Tommy brought up. That was undoubtedly why Clint felt so shut out of whatever Tommy was going through now over Sierra and the accident.

Still, Tommy's attitude toward Sierra made no sense at all. How could the boy not like her? *Why* didn't he like her? And why in God's name did he resent her staying on the ranch so much?

Clint managed enough normal conversation during the drive to fool Rosie, but deep down he wasn't fooling him-

self. He would never, not for the rest of his days, be able
to completely abolish Sierra from his thoughts. Physically
he was on his way to Hillman and the high school audi-
torium, but his heart was still at the ranch with Sierra.

What would she do all evening, alone in that big house?

What Sierra was doing surprised even herself. She had
wondered if she could sketch faces as well as she could
inanimate objects, and the drawing she made of Clint's
handsome features was so accurate it took her breath away.
What startled her most was that she had completely cap-
tured his personality. His kindness and intelligence was in
his eyes, and his sensuality showed in the lines of his
mouth.

She was good, she realized—not an amateur fooling
around with a pad and pencil, but a true artist. That exciting
conclusion raised some intriguing questions. Had she been
going to Cougar Mountain to do some work with the incredible scenery? Had there been art supplies in her van?

She was suddenly unnerved and distraught again. Who
was she? Did she have a reputation in the art world? Had
she earned her living with paints and pencils? Was there
any way to find out? Even if she contacted Montana art
galleries for information, would she learn anything when
she wasn't sure her name was Sierra?

After pondering it all for a long time, she gathered her
sketches, took them to her room and went to bed. Without
Clint on the ranch, she felt its isolation and silence. Without
Clint she felt lost and alone. He was her lifeline, her
strength, and she loved him.

But what if she was married and in love with her husband?

It took a while, but she eventually fell into a fitful sleep.

Clint and Rosie crept quietly into the house so they
wouldn't disturb Sierra, should she be sleeping.

"Good night," Rosie whispered, leaving Clint at the foot of the stairs.

"Good night, Rosie." Slowly Clint went up to his room. He felt weighted down with concern for Sierra and Tommy, and suspected he wouldn't sleep well with so much on his mind. But it was late, his body was tired and there was nothing to do but go to bed.

About an hour after retiring, Clint became annoyed at his restless rolling and tossing and got up again. He yanked on the pants he'd tossed on a chair when undressing and headed for the kitchen, thinking that a cup of cocoa might settle him down. It took only a few minutes to prepare the cocoa, then he carried the large mug out of the kitchen with the intention of drinking it in his office.

He was almost there when he heard something that stopped him in his tracks. Whimpering, moans and other disturbing sounds were coming from Sierra's room! He set the mug on a narrow table in the hall and ran to her door. Without even slowing down, he turned the knob and went in.

The room was dark, but there was enough light in the hall that he could see Sierra thrashing around in bed. Obviously she was in the throes of a bad dream. Clint shut the door and rushed over to the bed to sit down and lift her into his arms.

"It's only a dream, sweetheart," he said soothingly. "Just a dream."

"Clint? Oh, thank God." Sierra hugged him. "It was so awful. I was in a dark room or building...and there were spiders, so many spiders...." She shuddered and snuggled closer. "I feel so safe with you."

"I'll always be here for you, Sierra. For as long as you need me," he added, because neither of them knew the duration of their relationship.

"I...might always need you," she whispered, so low he just barely heard her.

His heart skipped a beat. Had she remembered something that *wouldn't* tear them apart? But even while he pondered that possibility, other things were overpowering his thoughts and questions. She was in his arms, clinging to him and telling him that she needed him. He could feel the silky fabric of her nightgown and the heat of her body under it. His desire for her was suddenly uncontrollable, and he took her face between his hands and kissed her mouth.

Sierra knew she shouldn't be doing this, but she couldn't seem to stop herself. She lay back and pulled Clint down with her, kissing him with feverish intensity. His blood pressure soared. He knew she wanted more than kisses, more than a feeling of safety. She wanted *him!*

He struggled out of his pants and got under the covers with her. Sliding a strap of her nightgown from her shoulder, he feathered kisses on her throat, her shoulder, the top of her breast. Her hands on his body, stroking, exploring, caressing, destroyed his last vestige of common sense. He worked her nightgown down past her breasts, and Sierra finished the job by tugging it down her hips and legs. So filled with emotion he thought he might burst, he cupped her breasts, brought them together and buried his face in them, inhaling her scent, drowning in the softness of her flesh. *I adore you. I love you more than life.*

He said nothing. Neither did Sierra. She moaned softly when he sucked on her nipples, and writhed and arched on the bed when he caressed her intimately. They couldn't seem to touch or kiss each other enough, and their need for fulfillment grew with the passing minutes.

Finally something *was* said. "Clint...Clint..." Sierra whispered hoarsely.

It was the plea he'd been waiting to hear, and he wasted no time in positioning himself on top of her. He was gentle with his first thrust, but then it became wild and wonderful. So that Rosie wouldn't hear—her room wasn't that far away—Sierra stifled her cries, but she truly wished she could let go of any and all restraints. She was on fire, rapidly reaching that magical moment of release, and it wasn't easy to express the ecstasy of her feelings in quiet whispers.

Clint, too, was striving for quiet. He couldn't prevent the bed from rocking, but he managed to keep himself from groaning too loudly. Such pleasure, though, he thought in the red haze of his mind. Such incredible pleasure. In all of his life he had never been more excited than he was with Sierra.

Almost at the pinnacle, Sierra pulled Clint's head down and pressed her mouth tightly against his, just so she wouldn't be able to scream when it happened. Still, when it did happen, when everything was spiraling, melting pleasure, she made whimpering noises deep in her throat.

Clint didn't shout or roar, but rode the wave to its crest with teeth-gritting silence. It lasted seconds, and then, completely drained, he collapsed on Sierra.

She lay with her eyes closed for a very long time, holding him, loving him. Again and again she relived the last ten or so minutes, and her clearest thought was that no matter what she learned about her past, she would not ever permit herself to feel guilty over what she'd done tonight with Clint.

He finally stirred, raised his head and tenderly kissed her. Then he whispered, "Are you all right?"

"You sound worried. Don't be, please. I knew exactly what I was doing."

"And it doesn't worry you?"

"I'm not going to let it worry me. No matter what happens, Clint, I will never be sorry about tonight." A tear seeped from her eye and slid down her temple. She was glad it was too dark for him to see it. "If you're sorry we made love, it will break my heart," she whispered unsteadily.

He felt like bawling and had to clear his throat. "Sierra, there are so many things I'd like to say to you."

"I know." There was a sob in her voice as she added, "Maybe someday."

Clint heaved a sigh and moved to one side. He held her close to his heart until she fell asleep. Then, very quietly, he got up, pulled on his pants and tiptoed from the room.

Eight

After a nearly sleepless night, Clint got up before the sun and drove to the Schulze Ranch. Tommy and Eric were already loading their duffel bags into the trunk of the Schulzes' car, so Clint was none too early.

He parked his truck, but before he could get out Tommy strolled over. Clint rolled down his window.

"Hi, Dad. What's up?"

Clint felt better from just looking at his son. Tommy was grinning from ear to ear, obviously in a great mood.

"Just wanted to say goodbye again," Clint said, mustering a grin himself.

Still grinning, Tommy bounded around the front of the truck and climbed in the passenger seat. "You're gonna miss your baby boy," he said teasingly, once the door was closed.

Clint couldn't help laughing. His "baby boy" was six feet two inches tall and had been shaving for three years. "Guess I am," he bantered back, then sobered. "I want you to have a good time in California, Tom, but you're going to be a long way from home, so keep a cool head, okay?''

"I bet you worried about me all night."

"Most of it, yes."

"Well, let me put your mind at ease, okay? Eric and I aren't going to do anything in California that we wouldn't do right here." Tommy grinned again. "Except for having the time of our lives."

"Which I want you to do. Only, like I said, try to keep a cool head. I guess what I'm really saying is be careful. I've been to Los Angeles, you haven't. The traffic is going to boggle your mind."

Tommy fell silent a moment, then said quietly, "You're worried I'm going to get into another accident."

Clint sighed. "I suppose that's it."

"Dad, I joke about being your baby boy, but I'm not a kid anymore. Are you going to worry for four years when I go away to college? I sure hope not."

"Sounds like you've decided on college. Which school, Tom?"

"The University of Montana or Colorado State. I have to send in my enrollment papers the day I get back from California or I'll be left out altogether. It's something Eric and I are going to talk about during this trip."

"Are you sure you're not already too late for this year's enrollment? A lot of schools close enrollment around the first of May."

"No problem, Dad. Both of those schools want me. Eric, too. We've got letters saying so."

"That's good news." Clint paused. "Tommy, I haven't said it for a long time, but I have to say it now. I love you, son."

"I love you, too, Dad," Tommy replied without embarrassment, which pleased Clint so much he felt that he and

Tommy were back on the best of terms and could once again talk about anything.

"Tom," he said quietly, "I want you to know something. Sierra has become very important to me."

Tommy spoke quietly, too. "You don't even know who she is, Dad."

"What I don't know is her history. I'm talking about the woman she is now. Son, I want you to think about something while you're gone. If Sierra knew she was a free woman—if I knew it—I would ask her to marry me."

Tommy stared at his father. "You like her that much?"

"I'm falling in love with her, Tom." Clint gentled his voice. "Loving another woman takes nothing away from the love I felt—and still do—for your mother. Can you understand that?"

"Guess so," Tommy mumbled.

Clint could tell how stunned Tommy was. "Anyhow, I thought you should know."

"What did she have to say about it?"

"Sierra? I haven't told her how I feel, and I won't until she's well. If—if she remembers someone else, I will never tell her."

"Jeez, Dad," Tommy muttered.

"I know it's a lot to take in, and I wouldn't have talked to you about it if I didn't believe in your right to know." Clint forced a smile. "I think the Schulzes are waiting for you. Have a good time in California."

"Yeah," Tommy drawled. "But keep a cool head."

"You know, I probably will worry when you're away at college."

"You'll probably still be worrying about me when I'm old and gray." Tommy gave his Dad a quick hug, then slid across the seat and got out.

Clint called a hello out the window to the Schulzes and then watched them and Tommy climb into their car. The two vehicles traveled the ranch driveway to the highway, then went in opposite directions.

Clint started the drive home, hoping he'd done the right thing by confessing his feelings for Sierra to Tommy. Two weeks was quite a while, anything could happen and he didn't want Tommy coming home to any surprises.

Clint noticed rain on the windshield and turned on the wipers, realizing that he hadn't even glanced at the sky this morning. As a born-and-bred rancher he'd been checking early morning skies most of his life, as his father had. As every Barrow who had lived on this land had done for generations. Forgetting the weather this morning wasn't a major oversight, but it told Clint something about himself: that he was more concerned about his son and Sierra than he was about the ranch these days.

He set his lips in a taut, thin line. He loved Sierra, and did he really give a damn if there was a man in her past? Even a husband? What kind of man would permit his wife to travel an untamed area like this all by herself? A man who didn't deserve a woman like Sierra, that's who.

Clint's thoughts began battling each other. The problem was that he could see so many sides to the situation, so many possibilities. He could tell himself all day that a husband who would let his wife take such chances didn't deserve to keep her, but deep down he respected the institution of marriage and the relationship between husband and wife.

It was a hell of a mess, that's what it was, he thought grimly. Sierra had proved how strongly she felt about him last night, but how long would those feelings last when her memory returned?

Sierra came partially awake, heard the rain and snuggled deeper into her covers. With her eyes closed she hovered in that cozy twilight zone between sleep and wakefulness. The bed and blankets felt soft as a cloud, hugging her body.

She was in a state of utter peace, total relaxation, and she made no effort to bring herself fully awake.

She had always loved the sound of rain, she thought dreamily, and suddenly there was a picture in her mind. She was standing at a window in a beautiful white bedroom, looking out at a rainy landscape. She frowned slightly, though her eyes were still closed, and subconsciously attempted to pick out details.

The picture dissolved and another took its place—a great body of water, with rolling waves crashing against a rocky shore. This picture, too, lasted only seconds before evolving into another: a sandy-haired man in a dark suit looking at her, then turning his back and walking away. At nearly the same moment a name flashed through her mind: Corey.

Sierra's heartbeat went crazy, and she forced herself to open her eyes and sit up. She took breaths in huge gulps. Had she been dreaming or were those pictures flashes from her past? Who was the man? Whose bedroom had she been in? Was the man's name Corey, or was Corey someone else? What body of water had she been near? Was it an ocean? And now that she was completely awake, how did she know that she had always loved rain?

A sudden debilitating weakness gripped her, and she sank back to her pillow, to think, to ponder, to wonder with a wildly beating pulse if she was beginning to remember or if those images had merely been disoriented dreams.

But they had been so clear, so real. Oh, God, what should she believe?

She was suddenly stricken with fear, and she huddled under the covers, quaking and shaking. She'd lost her memory; was she also losing her mind? Her grip on reality? Look what she'd done last night with Clint. And she'd felt no guilt over it, either.

She was feeling guilt now, and regret over her brazen behavior. Added to the fear chilling her system, the guilt and remorse made a deadly mixture of emotions. She wouldn't even permit herself to think about loving Clint. She could be a married woman. Maybe that sandy-haired man was her husband.

But if he was, where was he? Surely she would have told a husband where she was going, and why wasn't he in the area looking for her? Contacting the police, raising hell of some kind?

She realized that she was more frightened this morning than when she'd been in the hospital and initially facing the fact of her amnesia. Was this the way her memory would return—in disconnected flashes that caused outright panic?

Sierra drew a deep, unsteady breath. She couldn't give in to panic. She had to get hold of herself. Forcing herself out of bed, she plucked jeans, a sweater and loafers from her closet, underwear from the bureau drawer and headed for the bathroom and a shower.

Clint sat down to eat the breakfast that Rosie prepared for him when he got home. "Seen anything of Sierra this morning?" he asked the housekeeper.

"No, but I've heard her stirring around. She slept in, I guess. The men ate at the usual time and said they'd be working in the tack room. They said if you wanted them doing anything else when you got back to just let them know."

"No reason for them to be out in this downpour," Clint said. During inclement weather, he and his men worked outside only if it was necessary.

Rosie had things to do in the kitchen and left Clint to himself. He ate his breakfast, then decided to catch up on some paperwork and went to his office. Before he set to work with the checkbook and some invoices, though, he phoned the stations on the ranch to talk to his other men. Everyone agreed it was a day to work inside, and the conversations were brief.

Clint opened the checkbook and started paying bills. He was in the middle of writing a check when Sierra rapped on the frame of the door and said, "Good morning."

The sound of her voice was enough to make him forget about business. He stood up and walked around the desk, immediately feeling concern when he noticed the pallor of her skin.

"Are you all right?" he asked, and put his arms around her to bring her close.

As always, Clint's holding her relieved her fears. She laid her face against his chest and breathed in his scent. How could she have regretted last night? Whatever nightmare fate had decreed she live through, she loved this man.

"I'm fine now," she said softly.

He tipped up her chin to look into her eyes. "But you weren't before this? Did something happen?" He hesitated a moment, but had to ask. "You weren't upset and worrying about last night, were you?"

She couldn't help sighing. "I think I was worrying about everything."

"All night?"

"No, this morning when I first woke up."

Looking at her beautiful face, he realized that her bruises and abrasions were barely visible. Physically she had healed incredibly fast. Emotionally...?

"Tell me what was troubling you," he said softly.

Tears filled her eyes. "Oh, Clint."

"Honey, what is it?"

"I...something did happen. I don't know if I was dreaming or remembering, but I saw pictures." She gave a shaky little laugh. "It sounds crazy, I know, but I was still in bed, listening to the rain, and these pictures suddenly formed in my mind."

He gently caressed her cheek. "Pictures of what, sweetheart?"

"I saw myself standing at a window in a beautiful bedroom, looking outside at the rain. I saw a huge body of water, and I think it was an ocean because of the waves rolling in and crashing against a rocky shoreline. I saw a...man.''

Clint became very still. "Did you recognize him?"

"No," she said sadly. "It all could have been a dream. I know I wasn't fully awake when it happened."

"But you really don't think so, do you?" Clint's heart felt heavy as lead. She was beginning to remember, and a man being one of her first memories was a crushing blow.

Sierra's lower lip trembled. "I wish I knew. Oh, Clint, how I wish I knew." She slipped from his arms and began pacing the room. "I've wondered if I should talk to Dr. Trugood. What do you think?"

"It probably wouldn't hurt," Clint replied slowly. "Do—do you recall what the man looked like?"

"Quite clearly. He was a nice-looking man with sandy hair, wearing a dark suit. Probably around thirty-five or so..." she said, knowing she was breaking Clint's heart and feeling terrible about it. But she couldn't keep this from him. After all he'd done for her, and considering the intimate turn of their relationship, she could not keep anything from him.

Clint was silent a moment, then said, "Yes, I think you should talk to Dr. Trugood. Why don't you sit at the desk there and phone him now? I'll leave you alone to make your call."

"You don't have to leave. I won't be telling him anything I haven't already told you."

"Have you had breakfast?"

"Not yet."

"Then I'll get you some coffee. Make that call, Sierra. The more I think about it, the more important professional advice becomes. I'll be back." He walked out, feeling a hundred pounds heavier than he had only minutes ago. She would not be seeing pictures of a man if he wasn't part of her past. A *crucial* part of her past.

Sierra sat in Clint's chair at the desk, feeling as burdened and miserable as she knew he did. But however disturbing her past might be, she had to explore every clue to uncover it, even random images that might be no more than a segmented dream.

After dialing Information for Dr. Trugood's office number, she placed the call. A woman answered, "Health Clinic, Gloria speaking. How may I help you?"

Sierra cleared her throat. "Is Dr. Trugood in? My name is Sierra, and I need to speak to him. I'm sorry I can't give you a last name, but—"

"Don't concern yourself about that, Sierra. Dr. Trugood told me about you and said that if you ever called I should put you through if he was in. Hold on, please."

While Sierra waited for Dr. Trugood to come on the line, Clint was answering the front door. It was Montana state trooper John Mann, wearing a rain slicker and a friendly smile. He was carrying a brown leather case.

"Morning, Mr. Barrow. I'm here to see Sierra. May I come in?"

"Of course." Clint took the slicker Mann handed him, hung it in the foyer closet, then led him to the living room. Questions raced through Clint's mind. Mann wasn't here without a reason—what was it? What did he have to say to Sierra? Was he bringing good news or bad? It was all Clint could do to act as though he wasn't suddenly a bundle of nerves. "Sierra's on the phone right now. Have a seat. I'm sure she won't be long. Would you like some coffee?"

"Sure would, thanks. It's darned wet and chilly out there today."

"Yes, and it looks like it's going to last for a while. How do you take your coffee?"

"Straight," the trooper said with a grin. He settled into a chair and set the case at his feet.

Clint returned to the kitchen, where he'd been when the front doorbell had chimed. "Who was it?" Rosie asked.

"The Montana trooper investigating the accident. I'll take Sierra's coffee in to her, then bring him a cup." He rushed out with a mug of coffee, walked into the office and set the mug on the desk.

"I'm still on hold for the doctor," Sierra said, reaching for the mug with her free hand. "Thank you, Clint."

"Sierra, John Mann is here. He's in the living room." Try as he might, Clint couldn't make his expression nonchalant, as though Mann's visit was of no import.

Sierra's heart began pounding. "Maybe he has information about my identity. Did he say anything, give you any hints?"

"All he said was that he wanted to see you." Clint saw anxiety in Sierra's eyes and hastened to reassure her. "Don't rush your talk with Dr. Trugood. It's probably every bit as important as whatever it is that brought Mann here today."

Sierra didn't totally agree. Her impulse was to hang up and place the call to Dr. Trugood again later. Trooper Mann *must* have information about her or he wouldn't be here. Before she could act however, Dr. Trugood came on the line.

"Sierra, I'm very glad to hear from you. How are you?"

Sierra sent Clint a weak smile. "I—I don't know, Doctor. That's why I called." She watched Clint leave and dragged her thoughts from John Mann waiting for her in the living room to the reason she'd made this call. Quickly, but missing no details, she explained what had happened to her this morning. "Doctor, my question is, do you think those images mean anything?"

"More important, Sierra, do *you* think they mean anything? Obviously the occurrence affected you or you wouldn't be disturbed by it. Let me say this. I've dealt with about a dozen true amnesiacs in my career. Every case was different. Each patient's memory returned in a different way. Several suddenly remembered everything one day for no rhyme or reason. One man's recollections began with childhood memories and expanded from there. My point is, Sierra, that no one can predict exactly how your situation will correct itself. The images you saw this morning could very well be a beginning. Did you have any sense of familiarity with them?"

"I can't say I felt *no* familiarity," Sierra said slowly. "But my uppermost feelings were fear and panic."

"Do you feel that way now?"

"No."

"Good. Sierra, I believe it would be beneficial for you to come in and see me. I'd like to delve into these flashes, as you called them, a little more, and perhaps we might try hypnosis. How do you feel about that?"

"Would hypnosis help?"

"I can't guarantee anything, but it might."

Sierra's stomach roiled sickishly. For some reason the idea of hypnosis was unnerving. "Let me think about that, Doctor."

"Whatever you say. But even excluding hypnosis therapy, I think you should be under a doctor's care. If not me, then another psychologist."

"I'll think about that, too. Thank you for talking to me, Doctor. Goodbye." Sierra put down the phone and sat there thinking about the conversation. It was helpful to have learned that her memory could return in any number of ways. At least if she experienced another onslaught of disoriented images, she wouldn't panic over it.

As for visiting the psychologist on a regular basis, as Dr. Trugood had suggested, it would be terribly costly and she didn't have a cent to her name. The state of Montana had obviously picked up the tab on her stay in the hospital, but she simply could not see herself applying for further medical aid. Maybe that was a foolish, prideful attitude, but she couldn't dislodge it from her system. Clint would give her the money, of that she had no doubt, but the mere idea of asking him for anything material, especially money, was too disheartening to even consider.

As for hypnosis, *that* idea scared the living daylights out of her. Why it did she couldn't begin to guess. Was there something in her past that her subconscious preferred she *not* remember?

Sierra put her face in her hands and groaned quietly. How much more of this could she stand? She couldn't let herself take charity from the state, but, getting down to brass tacks, wasn't she accepting charity from Clint? She couldn't do that for the rest of her life, so if she didn't recover soon, what was going to become of her? The past was a blank and she had no future until she discovered who she was. She was trapped in the present, she realized.

She knew Clint was worried about the sandy-haired man she'd envisioned this morning, and so was she. Yes, he could be a brother, a friend, maybe even her employer, but she suspected he was more, just as Clint did.

Sighing heavily, she got to her feet. Maybe John Mann had learned something that would help identify her. If she just knew her full name, for instance, things would start falling into place, wouldn't they?

Smoothing back her hair, Sierra left the office and went to the living room. Both men stood up as she walked in.

"Hello," she said to Trooper Mann.

"Hello, Sierra. You're looking well."

Sierra took a chair, and Clint and the policeman sat down again. "Physically I'm doing well, Officer Mann, but I still can't remember anything." She saw no good reason to mention this morning's disturbing occurrence, as she still wasn't convinced what it was—memory or dream.

"Sorry to hear that. Maybe the information I brought along will be of some help." Mann lifted his case to his lap and opened it.

Clint spoke. "Would you like me to leave you two alone?"

John Mann looked up. "I'll leave that up to Sierra."

"No, please, I'd like you to stay, Clint," she said quickly. There was a twinge of excitement within her at Mann's mention of information. Anything he could tell her about herself, anything at all, might be helpful.

Mann took out a small sheaf of papers. "This is the report from the FBI regarding your fingerprints."

Sierra's breath caught in her throat, but she said nothing.

"You're not on file, Sierra," the trooper said. "In other words, they have no record of your fingerprints."

Sierra frowned. "I guess I'm ignorant of procedure, but is that good or bad?"

"Well, for one thing it means you've never been arrested." Mann grinned at her. "That's good news, wouldn't you say?"

"Yes," she murmured.

"It also means you've never worked in law enforcement—in any civil servant's position, for that matter—nor have you ever been in the armed forces. In some states, such as Nevada, certain jobs require fingerprinting and registration with the state. Any job in gaming, for example. This report eliminates that probability."

Sierra's head was spinning. Mann was telling her what she hadn't done to earn a living. Did he have any information about what she *had* done?

John Mann returned the papers to the case and then took out a plastic bag. He set his case on the floor again, got up and walked over to Sierra. Opening the top of the bag, he held it out to her.

"Smell it," he told her.

Frowning slightly because she was puzzled, she took the small bag. It looked to her as though it contained bits and pieces of oily rags. Sniffing it, she quickly turned her head.

"It's a pungent odor," she said. "What is it?"

"Turpentine. Chemical symbol $C_{10}H_{16}$, an extremely volatile oil used in paints, varnishes and medicines." John took the bag from her hand, resealed the top of it and returned to his chair. "Sierra, a lot of the debris recovered from the wreckage along the bank of the river has this same odor. You were obviously carrying a supply of turpentine in your van. I'm sure you weren't mixing some kind of medicine with it, so I have to deduce you used it in your work, hobby or what have you. My own personal opinion is that you're an artist. You used oil paints, which require turpentine to clean brushes and other tools of the trade. Does that opinion ring any bells?"

Clint was staring at Sierra. "Rosie believes you're an artist, too."

"I—I've suspected it," Sierra said slowly.

"Let's go one step further," John Mann said. "According to Tommy and Eric, there were two explosions. I think one of them, the first, was the turpentine. The second, in that case, would have been the gas tank. You see, your vehicle somersaulted down that ravine. The turpentine probably overturned, the containers got damaged, or something happened to cause the volatile oil to saturate the interior of the van. A spark of metal against rock or something electrical started the fire. The turpentine exploded, spreading the fire to the gas tank. It was the second explosion that destroyed your vehicle so completely. The really frustrating part of it all is that if the accident had occurred anywhere else, we would already have found parts and pieces of the van that would identify it, and subsequently you, its owner. But the river's so high and wild at this time of the year that anything of value in that regard could have been washed miles downstream."

"Does that mean nothing that might lead to my identity will ever be recovered?" Sierra asked anxiously.

"No, not at all. Eventually the river will subside—it does the same thing every year. In the meantime, we're working on it. I've got men walking the bank of the river, just in case something got hung up in a crack or crevice, which Clint here can tell you is entirely possible.''

Officer Mann talked about the investigation for a few more minutes, mentioning that there was still no news of a missing person. Then he took his case and rain slicker and left.

Sierra and Clint looked at each other. "Did he tell me anything important?" she asked in a tremulous voice.

"I don't know, honey. I do know one thing, though. Go and get a jacket. We're driving to Missoula."

Sierra's eyes widened. "What for?"

"To buy you some art supplies."

Nine

Clint and Sierra did not discuss John Mann's information during the drive to Missoula. They each mulled it over in their thoughts, but as if by mutual agreement, neither brought it up. They didn't talk about the sandy-haired man either, although each of them was convinced that he was someone Sierra knew. What he meant to her was a question that lurked in both of their minds, but what good would talking about it do? Clint didn't even ask Sierra about her conversation with Dr. Trugood, although he couldn't help being curious about it.

Instead, they discussed the rain—which seemed to be abating the closer they got to Missoula—Tommy's two weeks in California, the ranch and other topics that didn't touch them personally. Each knew the other felt weighted down with concern, fearful of what might happen to their relationship once Sierra remembered everything, so they did the only thing they could do for now: they left it alone.

In the arts-and-crafts store, Sierra nearly swooned with

excitement, actually forgetting her problems in the thrill of choosing supplies. She figured she was functioning on instinct, because she knew exactly what to buy. It wasn't cheap. The final tab was over four hundred dollars, and when they left the store carrying her purchases, she came back to earth and felt downright disgusted with herself. She should *not* have permitted Clint to spend so much money on something that could turn out to be no more than a frivolous idea, even if she did suspect otherwise. Besides, four hundred dollars would probably pay for quite a few sessions with Dr. Trugood. Obviously her sense of priorities was as confused as everything else going on in her life.

"Clint," she said as they got in the truck, "I'm going to repay you. Right now I don't know how or when, but someday I'm going to reimburse you."

"Don't even think it," he said calmly.

"Please don't take that attitude," she said, sounding miserable. "For my own peace of mind, I *have* to believe that one day I will be able to pay my own way."

He saw on her face just how serious this was to her, so he relented. "All right, fine. Reimburse me if you want, only please don't worry about it." He started the truck. "Let's have dinner before we start back. I'll call Rosie and let her know."

Sierra realized that she hadn't eaten all day and her stomach was growling. So much had happened, and food had not entered her mind.

"You've got my vote on that idea," she said. "I'm starving."

"Thought you might be."

Clint took her to a very nice restaurant. They ate pasta with a delicious creamy sauce, grilled chicken and Caesar salad. Sierra wanted to tell Clint again that someday she would repay him for the art supplies, as well as for the clothes he'd bought her, but it wasn't a comfortable subject, so she kept her resolutions to herself and talked about food.

"I love pasta, don't you?" she said.

"Sometimes," Clint replied. "This dish is especially good."

"What's your favorite food?"

"I'm not sure I have a favorite. I like Rosie's meat loaf a lot. Actually I like almost everything she cooks."

"Rosie's a good cook, all right." Sierra was eating away when she said, "One of my favorites is crab salad." It took a moment, but what she'd just said finally registered. She stopped eating, lowered her fork and looked across the table into Clint's eyes. "It—it's something I've made," she said in a near whisper. "Many times."

There was a pregnant pause, then Clint said softly. "Tell me about your crab salad, Sierra."

Although she became paler by the second, Sierra recited the ingredients. When she was finished with the recipe, she said tremulously, "I *am* beginning to remember, aren't I?"

With their gazes locked on each other, Clint slowly nodded. "It appears so."

It was an incredibly emotional moment. Sierra's memory was returning, and what would be the consequences? For her, Clint had never looked handsomer, maybe because of the caring expression on his face as he looked at her. She thought of their lovemaking, the beauty and wonder of it, and wished with all her heart that she knew if she had ever felt this way about any other man.

Clint drew a breath that wasn't completely steady and asked, "Would you like dessert?"

She blinked, as though coming out of a trance. "No…no, thank you."

"Then let's get out of here." He turned his head to locate their waiter and beckoned him over.

After taking care of the check, they left. Clint laid his arm across her shoulders, and she leaned her head against him for the walk across the parking lot to his truck. The rain had stopped, the air was cool and fresh and it had grown dark while they were in the restaurant.

Once settled in the truck, Clint put his arms around her, and again she laid her head on his chest. *I love you,* she thought. *I love you so very much.* Sighing, she said nothing.

Clint's thoughts were virtually the same. He could think it, but he had no right to say it. He gently caressed her hair. "You have the most beautiful hair I've ever seen."

He didn't kiss her, feeling that if he kissed her once he might never stop. Heaving a sigh, he let go of her and started the engine. Sierra moved over and hooked her seat belt. They started the drive back to the ranch.

For a long time neither spoke. Their thoughts were heavy, ponderous and disheartening. Sierra finally broke the silence.

"Dr. Trugood said that an amnesiac's memory could return in any number of ways. He wasn't alarmed that mine seems to be coming back in fragmented images," she said.

Clint was glad that she'd finally brought it up. "Did he suggest anything to help you along?"

Sierra hesitated a moment, then murmured, "Hypnosis."

Clint sent her a startled glance. "He thinks hypnosis would help?"

"There are no guarantees. He said it *might* help. I told him I would think about it."

"You don't like the idea."

"It scares me. Don't ask me why, because I don't know." She turned her head to look at Clint. "When I think of being hypnotized, I get this sense of—of a loss of control, and it's frightening. Is that childish of me?"

"Nothing about you is childish. You're entitled to any and every opinion you have." After a moment, Clint added, "*Are* you going to think about it?"

Sierra sighed and faced front again. "I don't know what I'm going to do. I—I'm not happy, Clint. Could anyone be happy in my situation?" She paused, then added softly,

"There are times when I'm happy. Every one of them has to do with you."

He sucked in a breath and clenched the steering wheel tightly enough to whiten his knuckles. She had just let him know how she felt about him without actually saying it. They were out of the city, and the country road was dark as pitch. Spotting a pullout on the right, he wheeled into it and stopped the truck. Leaving the engine idling, he slid over, unlatched Sierra's seat belt and pulled her into his arms.

"I want you happy *all* the time," he said almost gruffly. This time he kissed her, and her heated response brought his emotions to a feverish pitch in seconds. How he loved her! Her problems were *his* problems. He wanted to protect her from unhappiness, take care of her, smooth every bump that might arise for the rest of her life.

With his heart pounding he looked at her in the dim glow of the dash lights, seeing exactly what she was feeling in the misty depths of her eyes. "There are so many things I'd like to say to you," he said.

She laid her hand on his cheek. "I know, Clint, I know. But don't say them, please. It would only make… things…harder."

He took her hand from his cheek and pressed a kiss to her palm. Desire raged through his body, but sex wasn't all he wanted from Sierra. He knew from his marriage that love—the genuine, lasting kind of love—had many facets. He wanted Sierra well and healthy, and standing at his side through thick and thin. They hadn't laughed together, not really laughed, because nothing had been funny since they'd met, and he wanted so much for that to change.

And yet he was afraid of change. He felt so torn. Their situation was the most convoluted he'd ever encountered. Basically a simple man, he was befuddled by the complexity of loving a woman who might become an entirely different person at any given moment. The more she remembered, the more he suffered, and yet he could not be so selfish as to hope her memory would freeze at this point and she would forever remain the woman she was now.

Clasping the back of her head, he brought it to his chest and closed his eyes. But he held her like that for only a moment, because an idea suddenly struck him. It wasn't one that thrilled him, but maybe it would help Sierra, and he knew so clearly that they would never attain the relationship he wanted—and believed she wanted—until she recovered her memory. As afraid of change as he was, he felt compelled to do what he could to effect it.

He shifted positions to see her face again. "I'd like to try something. You were on your way to Cougar Mountain that day. Why don't I take you there tomorrow? You could bring your paints and things. I'll have Rosie pack us a lunch. You were going there for a reason. Maybe you'll remember what it was."

"Clint, that's a wonderful idea," Sierra exclaimed. "I've wondered so many times why I was on that road. Maybe I will remember something." She was becoming excited by the prospect. "Clint, what if we construct that day? Where was I coming *from?* Have you asked yourself that question? I have, many times. It was early morning, and I must have stayed the night somewhere."

"Unless you had equipment in your van to camp out," Clint said quietly.

Sierra's spirit deflated. "That's true, isn't it? For a minute there I thought I was on to something." She thought a moment. "Clint, would you think a woman would camp alone just anywhere? Are there any campgrounds in the area?"

"Yes, but most of them are off the beaten path. Sierra, my ranch is right on the edge of the Selway-Bitterroot Wilderness, which is more than a million acres of rugged, primitive country that straddles the Idaho-Montana border. Wildlife is abundant, including some grizzly bears. Think hard. Can you see yourself sleeping in a tent in an isolated place in that sort of country?''

"Maybe…maybe I slept in the van.''

"That's possible.''

Sierra heaved a dispirited sigh. "That's the problem—there are so *many* possibilities.''

"Let's go to Cougar Mountain tomorrow, and if that doesn't ring any bells, we'll explore some of those possibilities the day after.''

"Explore how?''

"Well, you had to have come from one of several directions. We could start by attempting to retrace your route. You know, stop and talk to anyone we might run into, ask if they'd ever seen you before.''

"Yes,'' Sierra said thoughtfully. "That makes sense. If we could find someone who'd seen me, maybe they also saw my van and noticed its license plate. Just knowing which state I came from could be a very big step.''

Although Clint's heart felt heavy, he tried to speak lightly. "We'll play detective, Sierra, and maybe we'll stumble across some clues to your identity.''

She forced a smile. "Maybe we will,'' she hopefully agreed.

Clint brought her close again and pressed a tender kiss to her forehead. Then he slid back behind the wheel. "It's worth a try,'' he said as he got the truck moving again. "Cougar Mountain tomorrow and a tour of the roads into the area the next day. Deal?''

"Deal,'' she murmured.

Before Sierra went to bed that night she sorted through her new art supplies. Almost lovingly she touched the tubes of paint, the brushes, the canvases. She'd chosen a breakdown easel, and she put it together and stood it on its legs. The light in her room was adequate for normal usage, but much too feeble to create a painting by.

She felt the strangeness of knowing so much about oil painting and yet not being able to recall even one picture she might have done. What was her forte—still life, portraits, landscape? Had she ever experimented with an abstract style? With art deco? She realized she knew the terms of the craft, but that was all she knew.

Sighing hopelessly, she opened the briefcase-size wooden box she had picked out to store smaller items in, and slowly filled it. Each tube of paint felt precious in her hand, each brush. In the art store she had examined and admired brushes that ran as high as ninety dollars apiece, then put them back on the shelf and settled for less expensive ones. All the same, she had a good selection and was eager to put them to use.

But not tomorrow, she decided. Clint's suggestion that she take her art supplies with her to Cougar Mountain had been kindly motivated but not practical. What she wanted to find out, if at all possible, was if something out there would tell her that she'd been to the mountain before. If she spent the day concentrating on that, she would not have time to do any painting. She was sure Clint would understand when she explained it to him.

Perhaps what made tomorrow's excursion most appealing was that she would be spending the day with Clint. The day after, as well. Without question she was looking forward to the next two days, even though she didn't harbor much hope of success. It seemed to her that her memory was going to return in bits and snatches, whatever she did to help it along.

Maybe she shouldn't discard Dr. Trugood's advice so cavalierly. Yes, the idea of hypnosis was frightening, but what if it unlocked her mind?

Sierra kept thinking about it while she got ready for bed. She realized that she had reached the point of doing almost anything to regain her memory. Money, or the lack thereof, was such an emotionally painful hurdle, she thought unhappily. If she did decide on hypnosis therapy, she would have to ask Clint to pay for it, but even if she promised to repay him a hundred times, what if she had no money? What if when she finally did remember her past, she found out she had nothing?

But she'd been driving a new vehicle, she reminded herself. At least Tommy had said it appeared to be new. That thought was encouraging until she started thinking that she may have bought it on time, in which case some financing company was expecting to receive monthly payments.

The van might not even have been hers, she thought next with a sinking sensation. She could have borrowed it, after all.

Fighting despondency, she forced herself to get ready for bed.

Nothing about the Cougar Mountain area nudged Sierra's memory. It was ruggedly beautiful, but to her vast disappointment felt as strange and unfamiliar as everything else going on in her life did.

Around noon Clint parked in a pretty little clearing and announced that this was a good spot to eat their picnic lunch. They got out and unloaded the things they'd brought with them. Clint opened a large sleeping bag and laid it on the damp grass with the waterproof-canvas side down. The lining was dark blue and fluffy, and very comfy to sit on.

Sierra unpacked the hamper, and they consumed the sandwiches and lemonade that Rosie had prepared for them. Sierra tried very hard to enjoy the picnic. The setting was incredible, with sunshine beaming into the clearing, the mountain air cool and clear, birds singing in the surrounding evergreens, the food delicious. And she was with Clint. In her present state of limbo, she could not have it any better than it was right now.

But her inner self, the part of her keeping her keyed up and on edge, would not relax. She was so weary of feeling that way that after stuffing the remnants of lunch back into the hamper, she stretched out full length on the sleeping bag and closed her eyes.

"I'm so tired of thinking about myself, Clint," she murmured. "Give me something else to think about. Tell me about you."

Clint lay back on an elbow. "What would you like to know about me?"

"Anything. Tell me about your parents."

"That's easy to do. They were great people. They wanted a big family, but I was all they got. Mother had several miscarriages in her younger years, and then I came along when she was in her forties. Dad was fourteen years older than her, so when I was sixteen he was almost seventy."

"And they loved you madly."

"They did."

"And you were a perfect son and never gave them a moment's worry."

Clint chuckled. "Not altogether. I remember one time when I disappointed them, especially Mother. I was on the football team in high school. The coach was a stickler for obeying the rules. He caught me smoking behind the school with a girl—a new girl in town who I thought was pretty cool. She smoked, and because she did and I wanted to impress her, I smoked with her. Coach came up on us and yelled so loudly I nearly swallowed the cigarette. He kicked me off the team right then and there, and I had to go home that day and tell Mother and Dad what had happened. Naturally I saw Mother first. Dad hadn't come to the house yet, and the minute I walked in Mother asked, 'What's wrong?' Guess she could see it on my face.

"Anyway, there was no way around confessing what I'd done. Mother and Dad never missed a football game, even those at other schools. I was so ashamed I could hardly look her in the eye, but I finally got it out."

"How did she take it?" Sierra murmured.

"Mother was an emotionally strong woman. I'd heard Dad raise his voice a few times—not at Mother or me, but if one of the hired men did something really stupid, Dad sometimes yelled. But never, not once, did I ever witness Mother losing her cool. She calmly asked, 'Do you have cigarettes with you now?'

"'No!' I told her, shocked that she might even *think* I was so hooked that I carried them with me. 'I've never bought a pack,' I told her. 'Someone gave them to me.'

"She didn't ask who," Clint continued. "What she did say was, 'Well, I guess you have to decide if you'd rather smoke or play football.' I remember mumbling, shame-facedly, that I'd rather play football. She nodded and went to the phone and called the school. She set up an appointment with the principal and the coach, and that evening all of us—Mother, Dad and me—met with them. It turned out well. I apologized and Coach let me back on the team. I never smoked again, but you know, it wasn't because of Coach's rules, it was because I knew how deeply I had disappointed my folks."

"And that's the worst thing you did growing up? No experimenting with drugs, no running around with wild kids, no getting in trouble with the law? Sounds to me as though you were almost perfect." Sierra opened her eyes and looked at Clint. "Maybe there weren't any drugs around your school."

"They were around," Clint said quietly. "Drugs were one thing I was never tempted to try. They're more available today than they were back then, but you could get them if you wanted to. Tommy and I have had many conversations about drugs. I believe in my soul that he's never fooled around with any variety of them."

"Then he's a good kid, too. Like his father before him."

Clint lay back so that he was looking up at the sky. "It has to be tough growing up in today's world. I started talking to Tommy about sex when he was eleven years old. I've never kidded myself about the realities a kid faces today, Sierra. Morals are looser and attitudes are different. A parent has to stay aware of the pitfalls and dangers his child encounters every day of his life.''

"Are you worried about Tommy being in California?''

"I'm not worried about him doing something he shouldn't do, Sierra. I always worry about his safety, wherever he is. I guess I can't help that.''

"The accident we were in must have been a terrible shock.''

"It was,'' Clint concurred. "I don't like Tommy using that shortcut over Cougar Pass, but—'' he sighed "—these are the roads we live near.''

"You know, a stranger to this area couldn't possibly imagine the many roads we've driven today.''

"You're right. If you stick to the highway, this entire area appears to be unpopulated. Even people coming out to hike and explore the mountain aren't aware of the ranches tucked in valleys here, there and everywhere.''

"There are a lot of ranches, then?''

"Well, they're miles apart and maybe 'a lot' is an exaggeration, but there are quite a few.'' It occurred to Clint that, for the first time, they were having a perfectly normal conversation. Sierra wasn't questioning her forgotten past; *he* wasn't questioning anything at all. It was incredibly pleasant lying on that big sleeping bag in the sweet mountain air and talking about subjects that didn't have dark, underlying themes. He wanted to keep it going, to maintain this normality between them for as long as he could, so he told her other stories from his youth. Some made her laugh, and he'd never heard a more wonderful sound than Sierra's laughter.

She was so pretty lying there, with her long, dark hair pooled beneath her head. Sunshine filtering through the trees dappled her jeans and white blouse. He suddenly ran out of stories, or maybe he simply stopped remembering his own past. The present was upon him again, and all he could think of was Sierra and how he would never find another woman to compare with her. He knew he'd been happy before meeting her, but he also knew nothing would ever be the same if she should vanish from his life.

He couldn't help himself. He crept across the sleeping bag to be next to her. She smiled at him, a winsome smile that touched his soul. Reclining on his elbow, he gazed down at her. "You are truly beautiful," he said gently.

"Am I?" she whispered. A female softness entered her eyes.

He twined a lock of her hair around his fingers. "Truly beautiful," he repeated huskily, letting go of her hair to tenderly run his forefinger over the features of her face. His hand continued to caress, traveling down her shoulder and arm to her hand. It happened to be her left hand, and he brought it up with the intention of pressing an adoring kiss to her palm.

But then he saw the indentation on her ring finger, and instead of kissing her, he found himself studying the unmistakable sign that she had worn a ring for a long time. Sierra watched his eyes become misty as a great sadness overtook her.

"I—I'm sorry," she whispered. "I'm so sorry."

"You have nothing to apologize for. But, Sierra, if you were wearing a ring, where is it?"

"I've asked myself that question a hundred times. Again, Clint, there are too many possibilities to count."

"I know." His gaze locked with hers. "If it was a valuable ring and you knew you were going to rough it for a while, you may have left it at home."

She sighed. "That's one possibility."

Clint thought a moment. "It isn't necessarily a wedding ring, you know. Or you could be divorced."

"Yes, I've considered that. But…" Her eyes slid from his and she stopped talking.

"But what if you're not. Isn't that what you were going to say?"

It took a while for her to finally whisper, "Yes."

Clint was wondering how much more of this he could take, loving her so much and having no right to speak his feelings. He *had* to find out the truth of her past, whatever it took. His mind raced, searching for a way out of this quandary. There had to be one. The police were doing what they could to unearth Sierra's identity, but what could *he* do?

Oh, sure, they could drive around tomorrow and attempt to find someone who had seen Sierra in the area, but that was such a long shot he didn't have much faith in its success, not when they didn't even know from which direction she had come.

He dampened his lips. "Tell me again what Dr. Trugood said about hypnosis therapy," he said quietly.

Sierra heaved a sigh. "He said it might help but there are no guarantees."

"But he would like you to try it."

"Yes."

"Do you think you could get past your fear of the treatment enough to try it? Honey, if you can't I'll understand. But—" he gritted his teeth "—I want you well. I want you to remember that ring. I want…so much…and if there's even the slimmest chance that hypnosis would help…"

He didn't have to say more. She knew exactly what he was getting at. It was time that she was completely honest with him on the subject of money. "Clint, seeing Dr. Trugood on a regular basis would be costly. I can't ask you to pay for one more thing for me. You've already spent hundreds and hundreds of dollars on me."

"My God, do you think I care?" Clint was appalled that she was so concerned about money. He'd told her she could pay him back if it made her feel better, but he honestly didn't give a damn if he ever saw a dime. "Sierra, listen to me. You and I...the two of us...our hands are tied as far as... You know what I mean. Damn, it's hard to say something without coming right out with it. But I do not want what I truly believe we have together to—to dissolve into nothing because of money. Do you understand what I'm saying? If you want to see Dr. Trugood every damned day, I'll pay for it. Gladly. And anything else that might help your recovery."

She probed the depths of his eyes. "I do understand what you're saying, but have you considered that we might not like what I remember, when I finally do?"

"Yes, I've thought about it from every angle. But we have to find out the truth, Sierra, we have to." He let the love he felt for her show in his eyes, and Sierra's breath caught in her throat at the intensity of feelings she saw there.

"I'll call Dr. Trugood and make an appointment," she whispered emotionally. "Clint, if it doesn't turn out the way we'd like it to..."

He gathered her into his arms and held her close. He endured the bittersweet agony for as long as he could, then gently released her and looked into her eyes.

"All we can do is hope," he said raggedly, adding, "and keep on trying. We can't give up, Sierra."

She nodded mutely.

Ten

The following morning Sierra called Dr. Trugood's office to make an appointment, even though she was still nervous and uneasy over the idea of hypnosis. But if it helped...? She really couldn't ignore that possibility, especially when, on her own, she seemed to be spinning her wheels.

The receptionist sounded harried and apologetic. "Dr. Trugood was called out of town on a family emergency, Sierra. I'm in the process of rescheduling this week's appointments, which, of course, is going to make next week extremely busy. But I know Dr. Trugood would like to see you. Let me do what I can. I'll call you back."

Relieved because she wouldn't have to face hypnosis for at least a week, Sierra recited the ranch's phone number and told the receptionist that she planned to be gone for most of the day. "If I'm not here when you call, please leave a message with the woman who answers the phone," she added. "Rosie will make sure I get it."

Clint was outside waiting for Sierra, and when she came

through the door and walked toward him, he heaved an
agonized sigh. She was more beautiful each time he looked
at her, and his feelings for her were reaching an almost
intolerable stage. He kept trying to remember that she could
be a married woman, but it was getting harder to do, especially when she looked as she did this morning in a pretty
skirt and blouse, and with the sun making her fabulous hair
glisten with highlights.

"I'm ready to go now," she said. They stood near Clint's
truck while she told him about her conversation with Dr.
Trugood's receptionist. "So," she finished, "maybe I'll
have an appointment next week, maybe not. I'm sure she'll
work me in if she can."

Clint noticed that she didn't seem at all disappointed with
this turn of events, but said nothing about it and nodded.
"Okay, fine. We might as well get started." He opened the
passenger door for Sierra, then walked around the truck to
get in himself.

Traversing the driveway to the road, he talked about
what they were planning on doing today. "Other than those
old logging tracks you saw yesterday, there are really only
a couple of roads that connect with the Cougar Mountain
road—the one from Missoula and a north-south artery that
wanders into the wilderness area. I think we should start
with that road, approaching from the south."

"Whatever you say," Sierra murmured. She already
knew that the road to Missoula wasn't familiar, although,
granted, they hadn't ever made any stops at cafés or motels
to talk about the possibility of someone having seen her
before. But she really didn't care where they began their
quest today, because she had so little hope of success. She
realized that she was beginning to accept her condition,
which was extremely unnerving, as the concept of never
knowing more about her past than she did right now
seemed so unjust.

But facts were facts. Maybe Dr. Trugood could help her,

maybe he couldn't. Maybe she would suddenly remember everything without outside aid, maybe not. Maybe John Mann would eventually identify her through police investigation, but she felt that there was an equal chance of her true identity never coming to light from his efforts.

She sent Clint a sidelong glance. What would she have done without his concern? His caring what happened to her? Where would she be right now if he'd taken no interest in her well-being?

Picturing herself completely alone, she shuddered.

"Are you cold?" Clint asked.

His question told her again how attuned he was to her feelings. "No, I'm not cold." Wasn't their emotional closeness rather amazing? Considering how short a time they'd known each other, and how little they both knew about *her*, wasn't this almost mystical rapport they had with each other *very* amazing?

"You're afraid we won't learn anything today," Clint said softly. His eyes left the road to send her an empathetic look.

She stared straight ahead. "I'm afraid we won't learn anything *ever*."

He tried to laugh. "Sometimes I'm afraid we will."

She turned her head so she could see him, and her heart nearly melted with love for this man. She had her fears and he had his. She knew in her soul that he wanted her to get well and was willing to do anything he could to help her attain that goal. And yet he was afraid of what success might bring.

She wanted to comfort him, as he had comforted her so many times. She wanted to say, "No matter what I find out about my past, I will never be able to bring myself to leave you."

But how could she make a promise she might not be in a position to keep? Misery suddenly overtook her, and she had to blink hard to hold back tears.

With the urge to cry under control, she deliberately brightened her voice and changed the subject. "This has to be one of the most beautiful days anyone has ever seen."

Clint agreed with a nod. "We're heading into the nicest time of year around here."

"Summer."

"Yes, our summers are pretty great. Our springs are usually rainy, anything can happen in the fall and winters can be brutal. But the summer months make up for the rest of the year." He sent her a wistful little grin. "Most of the time, anyhow."

"In other words, good summer weather isn't a given."

"Not always."

"But you love it here."

"It's my home, Sierra. I can't imagine living anywhere else."

Neither could she, she thought with an inner sigh. She *had* been in other places, though—in a large house with a fabulous white bedroom, for instance, and near an ocean. Maybe those two memories were connected. Maybe the large house faced an ocean, and she had been accustomed to watching a rolling sea.

Her thoughts returned to the immediate present. "Clint, do you think there's really a chance of those men finding an identifiable piece of my van with the river so high?"

"Yes, it's possible. The water is moving so fast it could throw even heavy objects onto a bank. Then, as John Mann said, things could get hung up in a crack or crevice along the river's path."

"I simply cannot visualize a vehicle literally blown to bits. The engine, for instance. Wouldn't it take a terrible blast for the engine to be completely demolished?"

"Well, it was a terrible blast, apparently. But you're right. I doubt that the engine was totally destroyed. It's probably somewhere in the river."

"Clint, if the engine is intact, wouldn't the river merely nudge it along? I mean, it's so heavy and all..."

"Honey, when that river's as high and wild as it is right now, it can move whole trees and granite boulders. Fast-moving water is a powerful force, Sierra."

Her shoulders slumped a little as she pictured the river rushing on its course for miles and miles, then emptying into another river, and another. She didn't know the geography of the area very well, but wasn't that what rivers did? She could ask Clint about it. He probably knew exactly where the water in that river eventually ended up, but did she really want a lesson on geography?

She approached the topic from another angle. "Clint, tell me this. How long will it be before the river settles down, assuming it does, of course."

"It definitely does. Sierra, the same thing happens every year. When the snowpacks in the mountains start to melt, the rivers rise. About midsummer, the water levels begin dropping and the rivers calm down. At that point, anything in them can be easily spotted by anyone walking the banks. The water gets so serene in some spots that the kids around here go swimming. Fishing is good then, and a lot of people go fishing. I taught Tommy how to fish in that very river, as a matter of fact."

"Midsummer? A good six weeks away," she murmured, as though her mind hadn't gotten past that one piece of information.

"Could be longer, depending on how fast the high-country snow melts."

She was thinking about living off of Clint for months yet, and realized that while she loved him, she wasn't at all comfortable with the idea of accepting his largesse indefinitely. She felt so damned helpless, and it was such an awful feeling that she had a sudden compelling urge to jump out of the truck and run. Her hand even went to the handle of her door and curled around it.

But it was a foolish, senseless urge, and she knew it. They were driving through tall timber, and she really had no idea of their exact location. Even if she didn't kill herself by jumping out of a moving vehicle, even if she survived such foolhardiness intact and uninjured, where in God's name would she go?

Vaguely she registered Clint turning onto another road. Then she realized it wasn't just another back road but a highway, and she stopped thinking morbid thoughts about night falling in that deep, dark forest and her being scared to death out there by herself.

She sat up straighter when she saw a small settlement. Her darting gaze took in a gas station, a restaurant, a small motel and four or five houses scattered among the timber.

"Where are we?" she asked.

"This little place is called Harrisville by the locals. It's not a real town and it's not shown on the state maps. A man by the name of Joseph Harris owns everything in sight. He bought the land about twenty years ago and built the gas station. Apparently it was profitable enough to add the restaurant and motel."

"And if I came in from the south I would have passed through here?"

"Yes."

Clint had been driving very slowly so she could get a really good look at Harrisville, but they were past it in minutes and he made a U-turn and drove back to stop in front of the restaurant. Sierra studied the squat, rustic building. There were three vehicles parked outside, indicating at least three customers. Had she stopped here for lunch, for dinner, for a snack?

She glanced over to the motel and wondered if she had stayed there the night before the accident, then at the gas station to wonder if she had purchased fuel there.

Her eyes finally met Clint's. "Is any of this familiar?" he asked.

She inhaled slowly, a sign of her bone-deep uncertainty. "No," she said sadly. She knew she could cry very easily right now, because it made sense that if she had been driving for a long time she would have stopped for a soft drink, at least, and there was nothing in her mind but confusion.

"Let's go in and have a cup of coffee," Clint said gently. He pulled the truck closer to the building and parked next to the other vehicles.

They got out. Clint took her hand and smiled at her. "Relax, honey. You might have driven through Harrisville without even noticing it was here."

"Are there any other motels between here and the Cougar Mountain road?"

"No."

"Then if I came this way, doesn't it make sense that I would have stayed the night at this one?"

He spoke quietly, soothingly. "Going south from here, there are towns with motels."

Sierra swallowed hard. "Meaning I could have stayed much farther away, gotten up very early and passed through Harrisville without, as you said, even noticing it was here."

"Anything's possible, honey."

Her lips suddenly twisted angrily. "That's what I hate about this...this miserable situation—all of those damned possibilities."

Clint squeezed her hand in mute understanding. "Come on, let's go in."

They walked to the entrance and Clint opened the door for her. At the sound of a cowbell clanking above the door, Sierra froze. Startled, Clint studied her face.

"What is it, Sierra?" There was avid curiosity in his voice. Was she remembering something?

But then she looked at him. "There was something about that cowbell...." She heaved a sigh. "Whatever it was, it's gone. Let's have our coffee."

They sat at a table. From his side of it, Clint could look

out the window and see the motel. After ordering two coffees from a young waitress, he said to Sierra, "You know, if you stayed at that motel, they would have a record of the make and license number of your van."

Sierra stared a moment before exclaiming. "My Lord, you're right! Why are we sitting *here?*"

Clint smiled. "Because they're not apt to let us go through their registration records. When we get home, I'll call John Mann. He'll know what to do."

Sierra was frowning slightly and biting her bottom lip. "Even if the motel operator permitted us to examine his records, what would we look for? We don't even know if my name really is Sierra, and we have no last name to go by. Even the law can't get past that hurdle."

"First of all, I believe your name *is* Sierra. Secondly, it's unusual enough to stand out on those registration slips. Mann will figure it out, bet you anything."

Sierra wasn't convinced, but she didn't say so.

The waitress brought their coffee and smiled in a friendly manner. Clint smiled back and read her name tag. "Brenda, may I ask you something?"

"Sure, go ahead," the waitress said.

"Have you ever seen this lady before?"

Brenda looked at Sierra, then shook her head. "No, can't say that I have." Her friendly smile appeared again. "Are you two playing some kind of game?"

Sierra responded before Clint could. "Sort of, Brenda. Forget it, okay?" When the woman walked away, shaking her head, Sierra couldn't help laughing. "She thinks we're a couple of nuts. She's right in my case."

"Don't say that. You are *not* a nut."

Sierra merely sighed.

Before leaving Harrisville, they talked to anyone they could find—the gas station attendant, the young man working at the motel, an older man walking his dog. No one had seen Sierra before, and without an explanation as to why they were being questioned, obviously they thought Clint and Sierra were a strange couple.

"I really can't blame anyone for thinking we're a weird pair," Sierra said with a sigh as they returned to the truck after enduring a very suspicious look from the man with the dog. "Amnesia would not be someone's first thought, would it? I mean, people might come to that conclusion, if they bothered to think about it, but they probably won't."

"Frankly, Sierra, I personally don't give a damn what anyone thinks." Starting the truck's engine, Clint looked at her. "Do you?"

"No, I guess not."

He followed the highway north and slowed down when they approached the Cougar Mountain road. At the intersection he pulled over to the side and stopped.

"If you came in from the south, that is the road you would have turned onto," he told her.

Sierra almost voraciously studied the turn. "Cougar Pass is on that road?"

"Yes."

"I was halfway hoping I was on that road by mistake," she murmured. "I can see now that it couldn't possibly have happened that way."

"Not if you came in from the south," Clint said quietly. "But supposing you were driving the back roads, some of those we were on yesterday, and got lost? Sierra, my point is we don't know if you were intentionally heading for Cougar Mountain."

She was silent for several moments. "We don't know anything about that day, Clint, and we're not *learning* anything by questioning strangers." She sighed. "You must be so tired of...of my problems. I know I am."

His eyes narrowed almost angrily, and he reached for her hand. "Listen to me and believe every word. I enjoy every minute we spend together. Okay, so we haven't made any great headway today, but the day's far from over. Please don't be discouraged, and never, never think I'm tired of the situation. Yes, I want you well, but it's for my sake as much as yours. Do you understand?''

His eyes were passionate with love. She knew it was for her. She leaned forward and laid her forehead against his chest. His hand rose to stroke her hair.

''I understand,'' she whispered.

They sat there, drawing comfort from each other, thinking thoughts they dared not express, until a car came along and broke the spell. Clint got back behind the wheel and Sierra straightened her spine.

''We're going to finish what we set out to do today,'' Clint said in a husky voice as he got the truck moving.

''Yes, of course,'' Sierra said quietly.

''This is the town of Hillman,'' Clint said. ''Over there, on the left, is the high school.''

Sierra craned her neck to look out Clint's window at the impressive brick building. ''Very nice,'' she murmured.

As they drove the streets of Hillman, Clint pointed out the sheriff's station and other places of interest.

''It's a lovely little town,'' Sierra said. She looked at Clint. ''There's something I'd like to tell you. I feel nothing here. In Harrisville I felt something, especially when we went into the café and I heard that cowbell. I don't know what that 'something' is, but I've been thinking about it. If I had to make a guess right now, I would have to say that I've been to Harrisville before. I think there's a good possibility that I ate in the restaurant and possibly even stayed at the motel.''

Clint returned her gaze. ''You feel that quite strongly?''

''I do, Clint. And I've not had that feeling on any other road. I believe I drove into the area via Harrisville.''

He drew a slow breath. ''That's a start, Sierra, a darned good one. Instead of waiting to get back to the ranch to call John Mann, let's go to the sheriff's station and talk to Sheriff Logan. Maybe it will take a court order for him to examine the motel's registration records. I really don't know *what* it will take, but Jeff Logan will.''

After a long, detailed talk with Sheriff Logan, Sierra's hopes had increased by leaps and bounds. He'd told them he would have no trouble at all in checking the Harrisville Motel's records, and that he would waste no time in letting them know what he found out.

They left the sheriff's office in high spirits. Clint threw his arm around Sierra's shoulders for the walk to his truck.

"I'm starving," he said. "There's a place here that makes great sandwiches. How about we stop and buy some, then I'll take you to the bluff to eat them.''

"I'm hungry, too. What's the bluff?''

"An overlook about five miles out of town. You can see the whole valley from there.''

"Sounds wonderful.''

Twenty minutes later they were leaving Hillman with a bag of sandwiches, some soft drinks and several bottles of cold water. Sierra opened one of the bottles and handed it to Clint, then opened one for herself.

"You haven't done any painting yet,'' Clint commented.

"Haven't had the time. Maybe tomorrow.'' Sierra was looking at the countryside. "This whole area is inspiring. It's really beautiful here, Clint.''

"You must like the outdoors.''

Sierra thought a moment. "You're right, I must.'' She managed a small laugh. "At least I do now.''

"Well, I have a theory about amnesia. Since I have no medical training, it could be miles off base, but I really can't see the condition changing a person's personality or character. We are what we are, Sierra, and just because someone can't remember beyond a certain point in his or her life doesn't mean they are any different than they always were.''

She smiled. "Whether or not that theory holds water, Clint, I like it."

"It makes sense, though, don't you agree?"

"Yes, it makes sense, but I have to wonder if there's anything at all sensible about amnesia," Sierra said wryly.

"Well, no one would ever be able to convince me that you weren't *always* the sweet, wonderful woman you are today."

Sierra's eyes glowed at his compliment. She took a swallow from her bottle of water, feeling at that exact moment as though the world was her oyster.

It wasn't, of course, and the feeling faded away. But it had been wonderful while it lasted, and had given her a glimpse of what life would be like with Clint as her husband. She was still contemplating that particular magic when they turned onto a sharply inclining dirt road. Her eyes widened considerably when she saw the drop-off on the right side of the truck. As the road climbed higher and the drop-off got steeper, her body stiffened and she tucked her bottle of water between her thighs so she could hang on with both hands.

Then she saw it, up ahead—a horrifying sight. It looked as though the road was going to completely disappear. They would go over the edge!

Clint noticed how she was sitting, one hand gripping the armrest on the door, the other dug into the seat. His heart nearly stopped beating when he saw the abject terror on her face. "Sierra, what's wrong?"

She never heard him. She was in a completely different vehicle, one with a blue interior, and she was doing the driving, heading for a blind curve, with a rushing river deep in a ravine on her right. Suddenly a red pickup came careening around the curve and smashed into her. She saw the river coming up to meet her, felt her vehicle bouncing downward, crashing into boulders, somersaulting.

She screamed. Clint slammed on the brakes, secured the emergency brake, since they were on such a sharp incline, and slid over on the seat.

"Sierra!" He pried her fingers loose from the seat between them and realized her hand was ice cold. "Sierra, look at me!"

She was breathing hard, almost panting, and her eyes were positively wild. Clint had never been so shaken in his life.

"Sierra, for God's sake, pull yourself out of this!" He took her shoulders and stared into her eyes, willing her to come back from wherever she'd gone.

In the next instant she collapsed against him, sobbing so hard her whole body was heaving. It was minutes before she could speak coherently, and he held her and did what he could to soothe her while he battled his own emotions and concentrated on hers.

She finally spoke. "I saw it, Clint. I saw the accident. *I remember the accident!*"

Eleven

Clint mumbled a self-directed curse. How could he have been so dense as to have taken her on a road with such similarities to the one over Cougar Pass?

He held her, rubbed her back and made consoling sounds until her shoulders stopped heaving, his mind working all the while. The road wasn't wide enough to turn his truck around. He could back it down to town level, but that might scare Sierra again. He had to go forward. There was another road he could have taken to reach the bluff, and it was how they would return to the highway, but for now, he *had* to go forward. It worried him, but he really had no choice.

Sierra's face was still buried in his shirt, but she had calmed enough to think about what she had remembered. Clint would want to talk about it, and so did she, but there was something about that awful memory she would never be able to tell him. It had *not* been a no-fault accident. Tommy had come around that curve like a bat out of hell, and he'd taken the curve so wide he'd been on her side of the road.

It was the cause of his animosity toward her, the reason he didn't want her at the ranch. She heaved a miserably unhappy sigh. Tommy was scared to death she would remember what had really happened that morning and tell his father.

Well, she never would. She would not put herself between father and son for any reason. Clint trusted his son implicitly, and for him to learn that Tommy had lied about his role in the accident would be a terrible blow. It might even damage their close relationship. No, Clint would not hear it from her. That was for Tommy to do. If he was of the same moral fiber as his father, he would not be able to live with the lie.

Clint could tell Sierra's nerves were settling down. He tipped up her chin and gazed anxiously into her moist eyes. "Feeling a little better now?"

"Yes."

"Sierra, we have to keep going," he said gently. "There's another road to the bluff, which is how we'll get back to the highway. I wish to high heaven I had used it this time, but I promise you'll never have to set eyes on this road again. But," he said, sounding regretful and a little helpless, "we have to stay on it to the top."

She didn't argue. "Do what you have to. I trust you."

When he moved back behind the wheel, however, she laid her head in his lap. He said nothing about seat belts. Her emotional stability right now was every bit as important as her physical safety, and he would drive very slowly, very cautiously. Besides, they hadn't met one other car, nor seen a soul, since leaving Hillman. Undoubtedly they would be alone up there on the bluff, which in his estimation was good, considering Sierra's present state of mind.

He felt relief when they reached the top, and he parked

well away from the edge of the bluff. The view was incredible, but he didn't mention it. If Sierra wanted to look
at the great expanse of valley, fine. If she didn't, that was
fine, too.

His heart ached for her. Apparently the healing process
for amnesia victims was not without pain. He could hardly
bear it; how could she?

He turned off the ignition. "We're here, Sierra, on level
ground."

She opened her eyes and looked up at him. He smiled
for her benefit and tenderly caressed her cheek. "It's going
to be all right," he told her.

"You're always there for me, aren't you? What would I
do without you?" she whispered.

He felt like bawling. He loved her so much, and this was
another perfect time to say so. It wasn't fair that he
couldn't, damn it—it just wasn't fair.

But she was beginning to remember, and maybe one of
her memories would be that she *wasn't* married or involved. It was the only consoling thing he could think of.

Sierra sat up. "Oh, the bluff is beautiful." Her gaze
swept the area and stopped on the seemingly endless view.

It didn't frighten her in the least, but she could tell that
Clint was worried about that possibility. She had to explain
her behavior on the road. "Clint, I'm not afraid up here. It
was reliving the accident that jarred me so much. I'm fine
now, really."

"Are you sure? Sierra, we don't have to stay here. We
can eat our lunch anywhere."

"Of course we can, but we're both hungry and there
really is no reason to leave. Please believe me."

"Do you want to get out, then? Are you positive that
you feel steady enough?"

"I—I still feel a little shaky inside, but it's not because
we're on this bluff. What happened back there was—*is* phe-
nomenal."

"Yes, it is. I want to hear all about it. Tell you what. Why don't you sit right here in the truck and let me find a nice spot for us to eat those sandwiches?"

"Really, Clint, I can help."

He laid his hand on her cheek. "Honey," he said beseechingly, "let me take care of you. I want to." She might be saying she was just fine, but her beautiful dark eyes were dilated and contained a strange light. He was functioning on instinct, as he'd never even known another amnesiac, but it seemed to him that the shocking experience Sierra had undergone only a few minutes ago would have a residual effect. Something to do with what he was seeing in her eyes.

"Stay here for a few minutes, okay?" he said with the utmost gentleness. "I'll get everything set up and come back and get you."

His concern was so touching that Sierra agreed. "All right."

"Good." Clint mustered a smile, then bounded from the truck. The sleeping bag they had used for their picnic on Cougar Mountain yesterday was still in the large tool chest in the bed of the pickup, and he was glad that he'd forgotten to put it away last night.

In no time he had everything ready in a pretty little spot surrounded by trees and underbrush. It was private enough that if anyone else did decide to visit the bluff today, they would not see Clint and Sierra eating and talking.

He returned to the truck and helped Sierra take the long step to the ground, then escorted her to their little nook in the trees.

She smiled when she saw it. "Very nice."

"Private, at least."

"Very." Sierra lowered herself to the sleeping bag.

Clint joined her and they dug into the bag of sandwiches. It was only a few moments before Sierra realized that her stomach was not going to accept very much food. Internally she felt like an explosion waiting to happen. Apparently the detailed memory of the accident had been as traumatic physically as it had been emotionally.

But she nibbled on a sandwich and drank quite a lot of water. Clint noticed she wasn't eating much, but didn't press her to eat more.

She finally brought up the subject on both of their minds. "It was so clear, Clint," she said quietly. "As though it was happening for real, instead of in my mind."

"What did you see? Can you talk about it?"

"I'd like to talk about it. What I've been wondering is why it didn't happen when you took me to Cougar Pass that day. Why, today, on an entirely different road?"

"Dr. Trugood might not even be able to answer that question, Sierra. It seems to me that these flashes of memory occur without cause or reason. It *could* have been the road, of course—a reminder, you know—but you're right. Why didn't it happen when you were actually at the scene of the accident?" Clint paused to take in a long, slow breath. Then he shook his head. "It's a tough one to figure out."

"It is, isn't it?" Sierra looked off through the trees to the edge of the bluff. Seated as she was, her only view was of the sky and a dusky configuration of far-off mountain peaks. After a moment she set her sandwich aside and lay back on the sleeping bag. Then, speaking slowly, looking up at the sky, she told Clint what she had remembered about the accident, everything except how fast and negligently Tommy had been driving on that dangerous road.

"The last thing I remember was unlatching my seat belt," she finished.

"You were knocked unconscious when you were thrown from the van."

"Apparently."

"When the boys saw the van on fire, they moved you to a safer spot behind a large boulder. Eric left then to call for help. Tommy stayed with you. Later, at the hospital, he mentioned how concerned he was about having moved you. Trooper Mann praised his quick thinking, which made him feel better. But you know, we've all heard so many times not to move accident victims for fear of intensifying their injuries.''

"He and Eric saved my life,'' Sierra said quietly. At that point in the accident it was the truth and she was very grateful. But there should not have been an accident in the first place, and there wouldn't have been one if Tommy hadn't been speeding.

Putting all that aside, however, she realized that suddenly remembering the ordeal—in great detail—was nothing short of amazing. Frightening while it was happening, yes, but still amazing. Her memory was returning. Not in the way she would like it to happen, not in any sort of sensible order, but in traumatic, unconnected segments. Where did the sandy-haired man fit into her life? Who was the person called Corey? Where was the large white house located? At least she knew what the memory of the accident was all about. The other things?

Well, she just didn't know, did she?

"Sierra, shocking as remembering the accident so clearly was, it's still a good sign,'' Clint said.

She hoisted herself up to lean on her elbow and look at him. "Yes, I know.'' He was sitting about three feet away, apparently done with his sandwich, and he returned her gaze with one that tore at her heartstrings. "I keep worrying you,'' she said in a choked voice. "I'm so sorry, Clint.''

"No, honey, no!'' He moved across the sleeping blanket to sit beside her. "You have nothing to apologize for. Please don't ever think you do.'' He took her free hand in his, and the warmth of his feelings traveled from his hand to hers and up her arm.

She was suddenly breathless. He affected her so strongly. Maybe she was particularly vulnerable at this moment, but she couldn't seem to deny herself the luxury of freely and openly admiring his good looks. His eyes were bluer than today's brilliant sky, and so filled with emotion she would have to be completely devoid of emotion herself not to notice. She knew he loved her. She knew he was in love with her. It was in his eyes, as clear as though he'd spoken the words.

And she loved him in the same intense way. Whatever fate had in store for her, for them, she knew in her soul that she would always love Clint Barrow. They might not have tomorrow, but they had today. For the present, today was all she had, one day at a time. She lay back again and held up her arms to him.

"Oh, Sierra," he whispered, and leaned down to kiss her.

Her arms wound around his neck and her mouth opened under his. Their passions exploded, and each knew there was no turning back. The self-imposed restraint they had lived with since their first time together had completely vanished.

Clint changed positions so that he was lying down. There was so much urgency in their kisses and caresses that within minutes he had her skirt up, her panties down and his jeans open.

Flushed with the heat of desire, Sierra spread her legs for him. He moved on top of her and almost roughly thrust into her. She gasped at the wild and wonderful sensations overwhelming her, then clasped him to herself by winding her arms and legs around him.

"You're beautiful, you're everything to me," he whispered raggedly, adoringly.

Their lovemaking wasn't tender or slow paced; it was hot and wild and a little bit crazy. But they'd held themselves in check far too long, and now they couldn't get enough of each other. She arched to meet his every thrust, and each one bonded them closer emotionally. No woman could love a man more than she loved Clint. Maybe she couldn't say it—maybe *he* couldn't—but they both knew it was true.

In the end Clint was as moved as Sierra. She kissed him and whispered "My love" too softly for him to hear. It was best that he hadn't heard, best that neither of them actually spoke of their feelings. If the day came that she had to walk away, it would be hard enough to do without vows of undying love between them.

But, dear God, how could she *ever* walk away from Clint?

They stayed in that special place for hours, making love or simply lying together and holding each other.

They did do *some* talking, of course.

"I feel pretty positive that you drove in from the south," Clint said at one point.

"It makes sense," Sierra murmured. Because of their repeated lovemaking, her body was so at peace she felt drowsy. If only they could stay here forever, she thought. Memory loss aside, had she ever been happier than she was right now? *Could* anyone be happier?

"And once Sheriff Logan checks those motel records at Harrisville, we're going to at least know your full name and in which state your van was registered," Clint added.

Sierra's pulse began fluttering in alarm, and her eyes opened. "I—I want to know, and yet I don't."

"I know, sweetheart, I know. I feel exactly the same." Clint drew her closer. Throughout the afternoon they had remained dressed, except for Sierra's panties, which he'd tucked under the edge of the sleeping bag. They were, after all, in a public place in broad daylight, and while no one else had come to the bluff so far, it could happen. He would not take the chance of embarrassing Sierra by lying there naked, but he didn't even attempt to keep his hands outside her clothing.

He loved touching her, running his hands up and down the smooth, silky length of her thighs, and upward to her tummy, her hips, then slipping them into her blouse to adore her breasts. But lying with her and caressing her that way kept arousing him, and when he felt it happening again, and then again, he marveled at the power of love. For years he'd lived like a monk and never thought he was missing anything. Then Sierra had entered his life, he'd fallen in love and his sexual potency had become astonishing.

How could he ever let her go?

It was a heartbreaking thought, and he shied from it. There was no way of foretelling the future, but they had the present. Making the most of it was all he could do.

He slipped his hand under her skirt again.

They were back at the ranch in time for dinner. Before they got out of the truck, Clint took Sierra's hand and looked deeply into her eyes. "Would you come to my room tonight? Rosie watches television in her room until nine or ten and wouldn't hear you on the stairs."

Sierra didn't hesitate a moment. "I'll come." She smiled. "Do you realize that I've never been on the second floor of the house before?"

"Then it's time you were. I'll close all the doors except mine. There'll be a light on." He brought her hand to his lips. "I'll never forget today."

"Neither will I, Clint. I think you know that."

"Yes, we both know, don't we?"

She nodded silently.

He gave her a smile and released her hand. "We'd better go in. No, you go in. I should go to the bunkhouse and talk to the men. See you tonight. Of course, I'll see you at dinner first, but you know I'll be thinking of later on, when we're alone again."

"Yes, I'll know exactly what you're thinking," Sierra said with a teasing lilt in her voice.

They got out, laughing, and walked in different directions.

Rosie greeted Sierra at the back door of the house, saying, "Sierra, you had a telephone call. A woman from a Dr. Trugood's office said to tell you that you have an appointment for next Thursday afternoon at two o'clock."

Sierra felt herself go tense, but she smiled and thanked Rosie. Sensing the housekeeper's curiosity, she added, "Dr. Trugood is a psychologist, Rosie. He treated me while I was in the hospital. I—I've been thinking that he might, uh, be of some help in—in furthering my, uh, recovery." Sierra knew she was stammering, but she had such mixed feelings about seeing Dr. Trugood that she simply couldn't speak without stumbling over the words.

She saw Rosie looking at her wrinkled clothes, and attempted a nonchalant laugh. "We did some, uh, exploring. I should have worn jeans today."

Rosie nodded, but there was the cutest little twinkle in her eyes, and Sierra suspected she hadn't fooled the older woman an iota with her explanation.

She knew it for certain when Rosie said, "I'm very glad that Clint is, uh, exploring again," then walked away humming under her breath.

Laughing under *her* breath, and overflowing with excited anticipation for the night ahead, Sierra headed for her bedroom to get clean clothes, then continued on to the bathroom for a shower.

Sierra tiptoed down the stairs shortly after midnight and entered her room as quietly as she could manage. Rosie might be on to what was happening between her and Clint, but Sierra still wanted their relationship kept as private as possible.

Without turning a light on, she slipped into bed and got

comfortable. Her body felt almost boneless. After hours of beautiful, sensuous lovemaking, Clint had fallen asleep. Feeling sleepy herself, Sierra had decided to return to her own room.

She closed her eyes, positive she would go out like a light. As she lay there in a dreamy state, waiting for sleep to take her, the image of a woman suddenly appeared in her mind. It wasn't a clear image; the woman's features were blurred. But she had blond hair.

Realizing she was undergoing another surge of memory, Sierra felt her heart begin to beat faster. It stunned her when the image expanded to include three other women. *All* of them had blond hair.

Sierra's hands clenched into fists from her intense efforts to concentrate. Who were these women—friends? Family? But she herself wasn't a blond, not even close. Her hair and eyes were almost black. Would she have blond sisters? Anything was possible, of course. Why wouldn't she have blond sisters?

But these women—she could still see them in her mind's eye, albeit vaguely—were not all the same age. One seemed much older than the other three—who was *she?*

And then one seemed to stand out, and Sierra was seeing her eyes, her nose, her mouth. Corey Mason! Oh, my God, she *knew* who Corey was. She remembered her! They were best friends!

But best friends where? And if she remembered Corey as a friend, did that make the other three women family?

Sierra's heart was pounding so hard she could hear it. Was the older woman in the vision her mother? If she was remembering her mother, why wasn't she also remembering her father?

She was no longer sleepy or relaxed. Her spine and legs had grown stiff with tension.

She lay there for hours trying to figure it out. Obviously

she was remembering the people she'd been closest to, so where did that put the sandy-haired man?

She wept, because she knew now that she *did* have a family and at least one very good friend. What if they were looking for her, worrying about where she was? If only she had a clue as to their own whereabouts.

Wait, maybe she did have a clue—that memory about watching waves crashing against a rocky shore. But there were two oceans, and hundreds, maybe thousands of miles of rocky shoreline, in many coastal states. Oh, this is so frustrating, she thought. A glimpse of her past now and then, when she least expected it, was a torment she couldn't possibly deserve. Why didn't everything just come rushing back?

The sky was beginning to lighten in the east when she finally fell into an exhausted slumber. Her last coherent thought was that she didn't even know how old she was, and that fact seemed so sad that she went from wakefulness to sleep with tears in her eyes.

Twelve

It was nearly ten when Sierra opened her eyes. It was not a good awakening; it took about two seconds for her to realize that she felt so blue and depressed that she didn't want to get out of bed. Obviously her state of mind had sunk to a new low, and recognition of that fact seemed to drag her even lower. *I can't go on like this, I can't!*

Seeing Dr. Trugood suddenly became crucial. She would do anything, *anything* to get better, including hypnosis.

She would not see much of Clint today, and maybe that accounted in part for her depression. He'd told her last night that he would be working with his men today, without so much as a hint that he'd been spending too much time with her. But she knew he had. Before coming to the ranch she'd sworn to not be obtrusive, and she had done exactly the opposite. She was a terrible burden, that's what she was. How long would it be before Clint got tired of her problems?

She cried for a while, then remembered yesterday with

Clint and how wonderful it had been. Sitting up, she wiped her eyes and chided herself for being a damned wimp. Forcing herself out of bed, she gathered clean clothes and headed for the bathroom, where she took a long hot shower, finishing off with a blast of cold water that shook the remaining cobwebs from her brain.

Feeling much better, she dried her hair and got dressed. She was going to make this a productive day if all she did was some housecleaning for Rosie.

When Sierra asked what she could do around the house, after she'd eaten breakfast, the housekeeper told her that if she really wanted something to do, she could dust and vacuum. "But you don't have to do anything, Sierra," Rosie added with a concerned expression.

Sierra sighed. "Please don't worry about me anymore, Rosie. I'm physically strong and healthy, and I need something to do."

"What about your painting?"

Sierra stopped and stared. She'd forgotten all about those lovely new art supplies Clint had bought for her. She put her fingertips to her temples in a weary, oh-give-me-strength gesture. Was she losing what little mind she had left?

"I would much rather see you outside painting a pretty picture than shoving the vacuum cleaner around in here, Sierra," Rosie said with a kindly smile. "It's another beautiful day, and you should be outside enjoying it. Besides, I dusted and vacuumed only a few days ago. If you really want to go over it again, fine, but it's not at all necessary. You know, I'd just love to see your work. I have the feeling you're a very good artist."

Sierra had the same feeling. Or she had last week. How had she let it get away from her? She was suddenly anxious to use those paints and brushes, and she impulsively kissed Rosie on the cheek.

"Thank you, Rosie. You are very good therapy."

The lift to Sierra's spirit was nothing short of amazing.

Toting her supplies, she first circled the house, hoping for inspiration to strike, and then, when it didn't, she left the compound entirely and sought open country. Following a meandering creek—it looked high and rather fast, too, she thought with some uneasiness, picturing the river in her mind's eye—she came to a place of breathtaking beauty. Between two groves of trees was a distant, snow-capped mountain. If she could paint a picture with the creek in the foreground and the mountain in the background and keep it all in perspective, she would consider herself a true artist.

She set up her easel and began working.

Two hours later she was so deeply engrossed in what she was putting on the canvas that she didn't hear Clint approaching.

"Sierra?"

His voice brought her back from the magical place she'd been. She turned her head and smiled at him. "Hello, Clint."

"Rosie said you'd gone off to do some painting. How's it going?"

"Take a look, if you'd like."

He walked up to the easel and viewed her work. "Sierra," he said huskily, "it's incredible."

She wasn't coy with her answer. "It is rather good, isn't it? Of course, it's far from finished."

He studied the painting for a while longer, then looked at her. "Honey, John Mann is here."

The bottom dropped out of Sierra's stomach. "He wants to see me?"

"Yes."

"Did he say why?" Nervously she placed the brushes she'd been using in a glass jar containing turpentine, then draped a clean white cloth over the painting.

"All he said was that he had something to tell you," Clint replied somberly.

Sierra's imagination went a little crazy. *Sierra, we know*

*who you are, and we've located your husband. He's on his
way to get you.*

Clint sensed her tension and put his arms around her.
"Don't be afraid," he murmured. "Please don't be afraid."

"I—I can't help it," she whispered into the front of his
shirt. Beneath the fabric she could feel his heartbeat, his
warmth. She knew his body as well as her own, and she
loved him with every fiber of her being. If John Mann was
here to finally clear up her past, maybe she didn't want to
talk to him at all.

But even if she convinced Clint to lie for her, to tell
Trooper Mann that he hadn't been able to find her, the
police officer would come back. There was no hiding from
the truth. She must face it, whatever it was, and live with
it.

And so must Clint. Her heart was breaking as much for
him as for herself.

But she stepped back, straightened her shoulders and
took a deep breath. "Let's go get it over with."

They walked to the compound holding hands. "This
morning I swore that I would do anything to get well," she
said quietly. "I swing one way and then another almost
constantly."

"I've been doing the same thing."

His face was haggard from inner stresses. Life without
Sierra would be empty, meaningless. Yet they were functioning in a state of limbo, which wasn't good either. Besides, even without police investigation and intervention,
Sierra was remembering things on her own. Eventually she
would remember everything. No one could change her past.
It was what it was, and if she was married, Clint would
have to accept it. He believed very strongly in the sanctity
of marriage and would never knowingly come between a
husband and wife, even if she was Sierra and he would
love her till his dying day.

They entered the house and then the living room with

sober, serious expressions. John Mann got to his feet. He
was smiling broadly.

"Hello, Sierra."

"Hello."

"I brought you some good news."

Sierra sank into a chair and John Mann resumed his.
Clint stood behind Sierra's chair, tensely awaiting the officer's "good news."

"We found the engine block of your van," Mann announced, obviously thrilled to be the bearer of such good
tidings. "It was about a quarter mile downstream, hung up
in a snag of tree branches, mud and rocks. Although the
block number was pretty worn down by water pressure, it's
readable, and the process of learning which company manufactured it, and which vehicle it was eventually used in,
is already underway. It shouldn't take more than a few days
to track it to its final destination."

Sierra's heart skipped a beat. "That—that's wonderful."
A few days and she would know her full name and address.
Or, rather, she would know the name of the registered
owner of the van. It could be someone other than herself—
maybe...maybe her husband.

A ponderous sensation developed within her, and auto-
matically she sought contact with Clint. Raising her hand
to the back of the chair, she immediately felt Clint's hand
close around hers. For a moment she marveled at their com-
munion. He understood as much about herself as she did,
maybe more, and he was always there when she needed
him.

If a husband came to light from John Mann's investigation of the accident, and she still did not remember him,
would she be able to force herself to leave Clint and return
to a home she didn't know?

"John, would you like a cup of coffee or a soda?" Sierra
heard Clint asking.

The police officer shook his head. "Thanks, Clint, but duty calls." He got to his feet.

Clint squeezed Sierra's hand, then let it slip from his. Walking around her chair, he escorted the trooper to the front door. They shook hands. "Thanks for driving out here, John."

The officer looked him in the eye. "Is Sierra all right?"

Clint hesitated. "Yes and no. Physically she's as fit as you and I. Her memory is starting to come back, but not in any kind of order, and it sometimes scares the hell out of her."

"She didn't seem particularly happy over my news. I thought she would be."

"Yes, well, she has a lot to work through."

"How's Tommy doing?"

Clint grinned a little. "I would imagine he's doing great. He and Eric are in Los Angeles. The trip was a graduation present."

Grinning in turn, John fitted his hat on his head. "In that case I agree with you. He's probably doing great. I'll keep you and Sierra informed. As I said, we should have some concrete information in a few days." He started out, then hesitated. "Oh, by the way, Jeff Logan told me that he was stuck as far as checking the Harrisville Motel's registration records. There's a problem there, Clint. We don't know if Harris is trying to beat taxes or what, but he doesn't keep registration cards on file for more than a few weeks. Throws them away. Said he doesn't have the room to store unnecessary paperwork."

Clint frowned. "That can't be lawful."

"It's one of those gray areas, and up to IRS agents to do something about it, if they're of a mind. I'll be seeing you."

Sierra could hear them talking in the foyer, but she couldn't make out what they were saying. She didn't care. She felt empty, as though her heart and soul had vanished.

She was sitting with her head back and her eyes closed when Clint returned.

He put his hands on the arms of her chair and leaned over her. "Sierra?"

Her lids fluttered open, and for the longest time they looked into each other's eyes. There was nothing to say, she thought sadly. In a few days they would know who she was, or at the very least, know the name of someone who could identify her. Until then…

She drew a long breath. "I'm going to go and finish my painting," she murmured.

Clint straightened. "All right. Honey, try not to worry too much."

She got up from the chair and walked to the doorway, where she stopped and turned. "If you can promise not to worry, I'll do the same. Can you?"

"No," he said in a quiet but strained voice.

"See you later." Sierra left with a catch in her throat and her eyes burning. Maybe she could get lost in her painting again. She truly hoped so.

Sierra could not fall asleep. The more she tried to relax, the tighter her muscles got, and as for shutting down her mind, forget it. Almost all of her anxiety was caused by the comment Clint had made when they'd talked a little after dinner this evening. "If your van was insured, Sierra—and knowing you as I do I'm sure it was—you or whoever owned it should file a claim as soon as John delivers any data he learns about the vehicle."

She had become very still. "Do you think the insurance company will replace the van? What's the procedure?"

"Well, since it was a no-fault accident, your insurance company will probably replace the van, and mine will pay for the minor repairs on Tommy's truck. Shouldn't be any problems with the claims, as far as I can see."

"I would have to fill out forms...describe the accident...swear it's all true?"

"That's about it, yes. A simple matter, really."

It wasn't a simple matter to Sierra. How could she swear it had been a no-fault accident when it hadn't been? By the same token, how could she tell anyone what had really happened? The problem churned around and around in her mind until she could stand it no longer, and she got out of bed, put on a robe and slippers and stepped out onto the porch.

The night was cool and clear. She sat in a chair and propped her feet on the porch rail, thinking that this was much better than rolling and tossing. Certainly she felt less tense outside than she had in bed.

But she wasn't solving any problems by avoiding them with fresh air, was she?

She looked up at the starry sky and sighed. It was, she feared, going to be a long night.

It was never mentioned by either Clint or Sierra, but there seemed to be an unspoken agreement between them. Until they knew her background—which appeared to be just around the corner now—there would be no more physical intimacy. They could look at each other with love in their eyes, but that was as much as they allowed.

Sierra spent her daylight hours painting—producing some excellent work—and her nights strolling restlessly around the compound or sitting on the porch until utter exhaustion drove her to bed. Clint buried himself in work, as well, and he was too tired by nightfall to do any wandering. They were each waiting for John Mann to show up again, waiting with aching, fearful hearts; the atmosphere on the Barrow Ranch was almost as gloomy as it would be if someone close to them all had died.

The weekend arrived, and so did Tommy. On Sunday evening, around eight, the Schulzes dropped him off, and he bounded into the house with his duffel bag crammed with dirty clothes. He was suntanned and stunningly handsome, Sierra realized. So like his father, almost a replica, as far as looks went.

Clint clasped him in a welcoming bear hug. Laughing, father and son pounded each other's backs.

"You look great, Tom," Clint exclaimed. "However much fun you had, though, I'm glad you're home."

"We really did have a good time, Dad. The best." Tommy spotted Rosie standing by and left his father to hug her. "Hi, Rosie." Then he saw Sierra, and his expression sobered. "Hello, Sierra."

"Hello, Tom," she said quietly. She expected to see resentment in his eyes, as she had before his trip, and it surprised her when she didn't. There was something in them, but she wasn't sure what it was. Shame, maybe? Chagrin? Remorse? Dare she hope that he had done some serious thinking during his whirlwind vacation? Adults took responsibility for their actions. Was Tommy an adult or still a boy?

Tommy turned back to his father. "Dad, I'm going to throw a load of these dirty clothes into the washer, then have a shower. Could we talk after that? In your office?"

Clint looked curious. "Of course we can talk."

Rosie spoke up. "Are you hungry, Tommy?"

"I could use a couple of your great sandwiches, Rosie."

Rosie smiled happily. "I'll have a snack ready and waiting when you get out of the shower."

"Thanks." Toting his duffel bag, Tommy headed for the laundry room.

Clint smiled. "It's good to have him home."

Rosie smiled. "Indeed it is, Clint, indeed it is."

Sierra tried to smile, but said nothing. She liked Tommy, or felt that she could, given the opportunity. He had not invited friendship before his trip and she couldn't count on his doing so now, even though he didn't seem to be at all resentful of her presence at the moment.

It struck her that she could be the subject of his talk with Clint, and her eyes widened slightly. More accurately, the subject could be the accident!

Oh, if only it were, Sierra thought passionately.

Rosie had gone to the kitchen, and Clint and Sierra could hear her humming as she prepared Tommy's snack. They smiled at each other. "She's really glad to have Tommy home," Clint said.

"Yes, I can see that."

They fell silent, looking at each other with their hearts in their eyes, restraining themselves from doing more. It was Clint who started a conversation each had vowed not to have.

"This is pure torture, isn't it?" he said, his voice ragged with tension.

"Yes," she whispered.

"We should hear from John tomorrow."

"That's what I've been thinking, too. He said a few days...and counting the weekend, tomorrow will be the fifth day...." Her voice trailed off.

"This coming Thursday you have that appointment with Dr. Trugood. Maybe you won't have to keep it."

"Maybe not...." Sierra's head had started aching. There was so much to think about, to worry about. Events seemed to be bombarding her, creating so much tension in her system that even her arms and legs felt stiff. Certainly she felt it in her head. Recalling the pain medication she'd been given in the hospital, once the doctors had established that her concussion was not that serious, she wished she had just one of those little pills. They had eradicated all of the aches and pains in her body and had also made her drowsy.

It was what she needed now. With one of those pills she would sleep, and she felt that she needed very badly to sleep. Her head was pounding unmercifully. It was all catching up with her, she thought—the sleepless nights since John Mann's last visit, the frustration she'd lived with since waking up in the hospital without a memory, the fear that constantly gnawed at her. Even having fallen in love with Clint was taking a toll. She couldn't let herself be happy about it when she didn't know if she had a right to fall in love with anyone. She really couldn't take any more—not tonight, at any rate. Clint didn't need her tonight, not with Tommy back home, and neither did Rosie.

"Clint, I have a horrible headache. If you don't mind, I'm going to excuse myself and go to bed."

He became alarmed. "What kind of headache? Do you think it has something to do with the concussion you received in the accident?"

"No, no, please don't worry about that. It's just a...headache. I'm sorry I mentioned it. I'm just tired. I...haven't been sleeping well."

"How *could* you sleep well?" he said with a touch of bitterness in his voice. "You've gone through so much, and it's not over yet."

His tone startled her. It was so unlike him, and it made her feel worse than ever. She and her never-ending problems were starting to undermine his innate good nature. It felt like a final straw.

"Clint, I'm so sorry," she said in a voice thick with unshed tears. "I've caused you so much trouble. Good night." Turning, she raced from the room before he could react.

He started after her, then stopped himself. Obviously she wanted to be alone. Filled with anger and frustration because he couldn't relieve her misery, he clenched his fists at his sides. How much more could she take before she broke completely? If Tommy wasn't home Clint would go to her room tonight, whether he had a right to love her or not. To hell with "rights." He *did* love her, and her misery was his misery. He was reaching the breaking point himself, and if John didn't show his face tomorrow, he would phone him and find out what in hell was taking so long. Sierra had been living on the edge for four days now, and in all honesty, it had been the same for him.

Enough was enough.

Sierra searched the medicine cabinet in the downstairs bathroom and found a bottle of over-the-counter headache pills. She squinted her eyes against the pain to see the fine-print instructions on the bottle, and read that an adult could take two to four pills every four hours, as needed. There were cautions and recommendations, but she felt that all she needed was one dose, and shook out three of the pills, which she swallowed with a drink of water. Then, in her bedroom, she changed into her nightclothes. Her head was throbbing so horrifically she could hardly see, and she crawled into bed and lay very still, awaiting release from the pain's unbearable grip.

It subsided surprisingly fast, and she actually felt the tension leave her body. She drifted into a deep and dream-less sleep.

While Clint waited in his office for Tommy to show up, he went through the mail, which he'd let stack up for al-most a week. It was just the usual bills, advertisements and trade journals, easily sortable. He had several neat stacks of papers on his desk when Tommy walked in.

"Did you eat?" Clint asked.

"All done." Tommy sat in the chair closest to the front of the desk.

Clint leaned back in his chair. "How does it feel to be home?"

"It feels good. The trip was great but I'm glad to be back." Tommy drew a deep breath. "Dad, there's some-thing I have to talk to you about."

"Go ahead. You know you can talk to me about anything." Clint was thinking that Tommy might want to discuss college. He hoped his son hadn't changed his mind about furthering his education, but he could hardly force him to go to school if he didn't want to. Tommy was, after all, no longer a child.

"First...how's Sierra doing?" Tommy asked quietly. "Has she regained her memory?"

Clint blinked at his son. *That* was the last thing he'd thought Tommy would bring up.

"She's starting to remember, Tom. John Mann's men found the engine block of her van downriver just last week. They're tracking its number to find out which vehicle it eventually ended up in. When they know that—and we should hear from John tomorrow—they will also know who bought the vehicle. What I'm hoping for, of course, is that it was registered in Sierra's name."

"And you would have her full name and address. Unless, uh, maybe she's already remembered that stuff. Has she?"

"No."

"Has—has she remembered anything?"

Clint nodded. "A few things, yes. Not enough. *Far* from enough."

"Did she remember if she's married or not?"

Clint's lips thinned. "No, she didn't." Tough as this was to talk about, he was glad that Tommy's attitude toward Sierra had changed. Clint couldn't begin to guess the cause for the turnabout, but it was relieving.

"But you, uh, love her anyway."

Clint met his son's eyes in a direct, open gaze. "Yes, Tom, I love her." He watched Tommy straighten his shoulders. He suddenly seemed more mature, years older, and Clint wondered if he should believe his own eyes. "What is it, Tom? What's on your mind?"

"In California Eric and I cruised the coast. We did everything we'd planned on doing for months before graduation. It was so exciting we hardly slept at first, then we got more settled in and did a little better in that department. But you want to know what the most exciting part of the whole trip was, Dad? We were on our own. We ate when we felt like it, we went to bed when we felt like it. If we wanted a pizza at three in the morning, we jumped in the car and drove around until we found a pizza parlor that was still open. Meeting girls was so easy I couldn't believe it. It's a different world, Dad, totally different.''

"I'm glad you enjoyed it, Tom, genuinely glad.''

"Yeah, I enjoyed it, but there was something bothering me.'' Tommy got up and began pacing the room. "Every damned time I had a second to think, there it was, eating a hole in my gut.''

Clint frowned. "I don't understand.''

"I know you don't. You couldn't know, because I lied about it. I lied to you, to the sheriff and to John Mann.''

A lightbulb came on in Clint's head. "You're talking about the accident. What did you lie about, Tommy?''

Tommy stopped pacing, lifted his chin as though bracing himself, and looked at his father. "The accident was my fault. I was driving too fast and I took that curve too wide. You can drive that road a dozen times and never see another car, but that day there *was* another car, a blue van, and there was no way to avoid a collision. I saw it coming, I knew it was going to happen, even before I hit that patch of ice.

"Before the 'copter got there to pick up Sierra, Eric and I talked. We were scared to death. Sierra was unconscious and bleeding, and we thought she was…going to die. We manufactured the no-fault story, thinking that no one would ever know the truth.'' Tommy hung his head for a moment, then raised it again. "But someone did know the truth. I did, and I found out I can't live with that kind of lie, Dad. I had to tell you, and I'm going to have to tell the police. I—I'm sorry.'' Tommy's voice cracked. "That's all I can say. I'm so damned sorry.''

Clint sat there, sorrowful and stunned. He knew now why Tommy hadn't wanted Sierra on the ranch. He'd been terrified that she would remember what had really happened that day.

Well, she had, and she must have remembered this part of the accident along with everything else, even though she hadn't told him about it. Because Tommy was his son, he realized with a heavy heart. Because she hadn't wanted to hurt *him.* And he was hurt, make no mistake—damned hurt.

This was, to his knowledge, the first serious lie that Tommy had ever told him. Clint slowly, laboriously got to his feet.

"I can't tell you that what you did was all right, Tom, because it wasn't." He sounded old and tired, even to himself. But it was the way he felt right now, like an old, worn-out man. Sierra could have been killed because his son had been speeding on a dangerous road. As it was, she'd been seriously injured. Unnecessarily.

"I'm going to talk to John Mann in the morning," Tommy said in a subdued voice. He looked close to tears.

"Yes, do that."

"Dad, will you ever be able to forgive me?"

"I'm sure I will, Tom. Not this minute, but...in time. I'm going to bed now. Good night."

Tommy's voice was hoarse and raspy. "'Night, Dad."

Thirteen

Sierra awoke groggy and disoriented. Her bedroom was white! Where was she? It took a few minutes to place herself and to realize where she was and why.

But that white bedroom remained in her mind, and she knew it was the same one she had remembered before. There were other images connected to it—a large house, a mansion, really, and Corey Mason. Corey's legal name was Corella; Corey was a nickname. Sierra could clearly see her friend's face in her mind's eye. Mentally Sierra struggled to remember more, but her heavy concentration caused the images she *had* been seeing to vanish, as did dreams or a puff of smoke.

The fact that she kept seeing that white bedroom, however, was proof enough for Sierra to believe that she had lived in that mansion, used that bedroom, possibly for years. If only she could place it on the map, she thought wearily. In a particular city, a state. It raised so many questions, the most crucial being had she lived in that beautiful house by herself or with a husband?

But if she had a husband, why had she been traveling alone?

When her head started aching again, she threw back the covers and got up. She knew in her heart that John Mann would be dropping in today with some answers. Her stomach roiled at the thought, but she *had* to have answers soon. Even Clint, as attuned as he was to her moods and feelings, couldn't possibly grasp how close she was to going over the edge. No one could.

She showered and dressed, seeing the strain in her eyes in the bathroom mirror as she dried her hair. Reality seemed to be slipping away from her, probably because she wasn't sure anymore what was real and what wasn't. Whatever she learned from John Mann today would be better than what she had now. She might not like her past, but she couldn't go on much longer not knowing what it was.

Clint had decided to say nothing about Tommy's confession to Sierra until his son talked to John Mann. It had been a difficult decision, because he didn't want to hurt either Tommy or Sierra when he loved them both so much. But Tommy was trying to make amends, to do the right thing now, and Clint realized that he had to give his son the leeway to do it.

Besides, Clint had a gut feeling that everything was coming to a head. It was all he thought about while he worked outside with his men. He had called John at his home very early this morning, and the police officer had told him he would be at the ranch around nine. Clint had asked Rosie to pass that information on to Sierra when she got up, then wondered if he should have hung around the house to tell her himself.

But he hadn't been able to sit still, knowing that John wouldn't be there for hours, and *not* knowing how long

Sierra would sleep. God knew she needed rest. She had looked ready to fall over last night, and she'd had that awful headache to contend with to boot.

No, it was best that he stay busy, even though he kept one eye on his watch and the other on the driveway.

Sierra walked into the kitchen at eight-thirty. "Good morning, Rosie."

"Morning, honey."

It was obvious to Sierra that Rosie's sharp eyes were missing none of the strain in her own. No one could possibly miss that gaunt, haunted look, Sierra thought.

"Sit down and I'll fix you some breakfast," the housekeeper said gently.

"Just a piece of toast, Rosie. I'm not hungry." Sierra honestly didn't have the will to fix her own toast. If it was left to her, she wouldn't eat even that. She sank into a chair at the kitchen table.

Rosie dropped bread into the toaster, then filled a glass with orange juice and placed it in front of Sierra. "Would you like some coffee?"

"I...don't think so, but thank you." Sierra looked at the glass of juice and wondered if she could keep it down. As much as she enjoyed coffee, it didn't sound at all tempting this morning.

"You've lost weight since you've been here," Rosie said worriedly. "Honey, you *have* to eat more."

Sierra knew from the fit of her clothing that she had lost weight. It was really only one more crucial reason among many for uncovering her past, accepting it and getting on with a normal life. But Rosie was right; she had to eat more. When the housekeeper set a plate of warm toast on the table, Sierra forced herself to pick up a piece and take a bite.

"Thank you, Rosie," she murmured. "Is Clint working outdoors today?"

The housekeeper clapped her hand to her mouth. "Oh, goodness," she exclaimed. "I completely forgot what he said to tell you. John Mann is going to be here at nine."

Sierra's hands began trembling. She glanced at the clock on the wall and saw it was 8:45. He would be here in fifteen minutes! Mann must have phoned. He hadn't called ahead of his other visits. He must have important information. She had to get control of herself before he got here—she had to!

Tommy walked in. "What was that you said about John Mann, Rosie? Good morning, Sierra."

She nodded numbly.

"I told Sierra that he will be here at nine," Rosie said.

Tommy suddenly looked terribly nervous, Sierra noticed, but her concentration was focused on her own nervousness more than on Tommy's. It took great effort to finish eating her toast.

Tommy leaned against the refrigerator. "I thought Dad would wake me up this morning. What's he doing?"

"I have no idea," Rosie replied. "He's out working with the men, that's all I know. But he told me to let you sleep." She grinned. "Guess he thought you needed to catch up. Want some breakfast?"

"Uh, nine o'clock? That's only a few minutes away. Mann could drive up at any time. I'll eat later." Tommy pushed away from the refrigerator and wandered out of the kitchen.

"Well, that's the first time that boy has ever refused food," Rosie exclaimed with her hands on her hips. "I hope he didn't catch a bug in California."

Sierra had an idea what was bothering Tommy, but it wasn't a subject she could discuss with anyone. She finished drinking her orange juice, then got up to rinse her dishes and place them in the dishwasher, feeling Rosie's curious eyes on her all the while. Obviously she was curious about a lot of things this morning, and why wouldn't she be? Sierra forced a smile, although she was sure it was a pitiful effort at best.

"I'm going to wait in my room, Rosie. See you later."

Leaving the kitchen, she heard Rosie muttering, "I wish someone would tell me what's going on around here." She sounded a bit put out.

Well, she would know soon enough, Sierra thought. They all would. Anxiety tore at her insides as she entered her bedroom. She had to know, she wanted to know, and yet she couldn't get past the fear, the dread. Why, she might be saying goodbye to Clint, Tommy and Rosie this very day!

Clint heard the police cruiser coming before he saw it. With a burning, sinking sensation in his gut, he left the barn and walked out to meet it.

John Mann parked and got out with a big smile and his briefcase. "Morning, Clint."

"Morning, John." It shook Clint that even though he liked Trooper Mann, he would also like to tell him to get back in his car and get the hell off his property. But of course, he couldn't do that. Whatever information John had unearthed about Sierra, Clint needed to hear it. And so did Sierra. Was she watching from a window right now, stiff with fright and uneasy premonitions?

He had uneasy premonitions, that was certain. But he shook John's hand and invited him into the house. In the living room, he said, "I'll tell Sierra you're here. Make yourself to home, John. I'll only be a minute."

He stuck his head in the kitchen and saw only Rosie. She looked at him with a sympathetic expression. "Sierra's in her room."

"And Tommy?"

Rosie shrugged.

Clint hurried down the hall and rapped on Sierra's door. She opened it, and before Clint could stop himself, he pulled her into his arms. He held her very tightly for a few moments, then tipped her chin to look into her eyes. There was so much he wanted to say but he couldn't get the words out.

Clint kissed the top of her head. "We'd better go. John's waiting in the living room."

Arm in arm they traversed the hall, but when they approached the living room doorway, they realized that Tommy was in there, talking to the officer. Clint steered Sierra away from the door.

He took a very deep breath. "Sierra, there's something you have to know. Tommy is—" His voice broke, and he started again. "Tommy is responsible for the accident. He told me about it last night, and he's in there telling John Mann right now. He was speeding."

"I know, Clint," she said softly. "I remember it all, but I couldn't tell you that part of it." She saw Clint avert his gaze and she couldn't bear him feeling so badly over something he'd had nothing to do with. She laid her hand on his cheek. "I don't want this marring your and Tommy's relationship. He's doing the right thing, Clint. He made a mistake, he's doing his utmost to correct it and we all must get over it."

"His utmost would be to apologize to you."

"That may be in his plans. Give him a chance, Clint. Forgive him. He's your son and I know you love him more than life itself."

"I know I'll forgive him, Sierra, but it might take a little time. It's damned hard to overlook what he did to you. You could have died in that accident. What did happen was bad enough, but when I think—"

She moved her hand to place her fingertips on his lips. "*Don't* think. I didn't die, and in fact, Tommy and Eric saved my life. They're so very young, Clint, and I'm sure they were scared enough to run and leave me there alone.

But they didn't leave me, they took care of me, and they called for help.''

"Sierra, Tommy *caused* the accident. You wouldn't have needed help if he'd been driving sensibly.''

She gave a small smile. "And you and I would never have met.'' A look of shock entered Clint's eyes. "You hadn't thought of that?''

Before Clint could answer, Tommy came out of the living room. Seeing his father and Sierra standing in the hall, he walked over to them. His eyes were pink, and Sierra knew he'd done some crying while confessing his lie to John Mann. Her heart went out to the boy.

"I told him, Dad.'' Tommy looked at Sierra. "I need to tell you, too.''

"No, you don't,'' she said quietly. "I remembered the accident last week, Tommy—*all* of it.''

Tommy looked startled. "And you didn't tell Dad I was speeding?''

"I thought that was for you to do. I'm very glad you did it, Tom.'' They weren't friends yet, Sierra realized, but they could be, if she was around long enough. She brushed away a tear, turning her head in hopes Clint and Tommy hadn't seen it. The truth was they were all so emotional right now that if one of them started crying, all three might end up in tears.

Clearing his throat, Clint put his hands on his son's shoulders. "I'm proud of you, son.''

Tommy's eyes dropped. "I'm not so proud. I'm not proud of lying, that's for sure.''

"Sometimes life's lessons are hard.'' He let go of Tommy and looked at Sierra. "Ready?''

She nodded, thinking that was the biggest lie ever. But it had to be done, and she let Clint take her arm and lead her into the living room.

John Mann got to his feet. "Morning, Sierra.''

"Good morning,'' she replied, marveling that she could

sound so calm when her heart was nearly bursting through the wall of her chest.

When she sat down, the two men did. John Mann lifted his briefcase to his lap, opened it and withdrew a sheaf of papers. Sierra held her breath. Glancing at Clint, she saw the same tension she was feeling on his face. He felt her gaze, apparently, because he brought his eyes to hers, and she saw love in them, adoration.

John Mann's voice brought her back to earth. "Sierra, I'm not sure how to begin. Before I do, let me ask if you've remembered anything of your past."

She dampened her dry lips with the tip of her tongue. "Just bits and pieces."

"Nothing about your family?"

Oh, God, the man with sand-colored hair! "I—I'm not sure. I really haven't been able to connect the dots, so to speak."

"In that case I'm going to start at the beginning." John Mann waited a moment, apparently seeking a reaction from Sierra. Seeing nothing out of the ordinary—other than her remarkable stillness—he looked down at the papers in his hand. "The motor block we found in the river ended up in a minivan, which was purchased by a San Francisco dealer. He sold it to a woman named Sierra Benning." John recited an address and telephone number.

Benning...Benning. The name went around and around in Sierra's mind. It was *her* name! Sierra Jean Benning. That big white house she'd been seeing was in San Francisco. She could see it clearly, the vast gardens and acres of lawn. There was a marvelous view of the bay from the property. Yes, she remembered it—remembered it very well! She clutched the arms of her chair as memory began flooding her brain.

John continued. "Once we knew your full name and address in California, it was a simple matter to gather further information, anything of legal record, that is. You were married to a Michael Findley seven years ago and your final divorce papers were filed about six weeks before the accident. There was another recorded document, whereby you returned to Michael all the property and assets you received in your divorce settlement.''

It was all coming back. Sierra moved to sit on the edge of her seat, leaning forward, her face excited. "He was called Mike, and he had sandy hair. He's a lawyer in the Findley family's law firm." Her gaze sought Clint's, who looked ready to jump out of his skin with joy. "We never had children. I—I'm not married, Clint!''

John smiled. "Obviously you're not unhappy about that. And you're remembering on your own now, aren't you? That's really great. Sierra, do you remember your own family?''

She thought for a moment, then spoke slowly. "My parents are...both dead. I have two sisters." She could sit still no longer, and jumped up. "I can remember! Oh, God, I can remember!''

John stood. "I don't think I'm needed here any longer. Sierra, I'm going to leave these papers with you. Clint, would you walk me out? I'd like to talk to you about something.''

Clint rose with his eyes on Sierra. She smiled. "Go, it's okay. I'm fine. I'm wonderful. I'm remembering!" On impulse, she dashed over to John Mann and threw her arms around him. "Thank you, oh, thank you!''

He patted her back and grinned. "Glad I was of some help.''

Sierra released her hold on him and beamed with happiness. "*Some* help? You gave me back my life!''

"You would have remembered it all, eventually.''

"Probably, but 'eventually' was really dragging its heels, John." Sierra couldn't help herself; she danced around the room. "I feel so *free!*''

"I do like happy endings," John said with a laugh.

"Goodbye, Sierra. I hope you're always as happy as you are this minute." He looked at Clint, who nodded. They left the room and walked outside to stand next to John's car.

John got right to the point. "Tommy's a good kid, Clint. There are so many who aren't these days. I might have to ticket him for speeding and negligent driving. I'm going to talk to my captain and get his input. The law's the law, but in special cases we can sometimes make exceptions. I think this is one of those times, but it's really not my decision. I'll let you know."

Clint heartily shook John's hand. "I can't thank you enough for what you did for Sierra, John. As for Tommy, whatever your captain decides, the Barrow family will abide by it."

Inside the house Sierra was undergoing a very disturbing memory. Everything she owned had been destroyed in the accident! She'd had thousands of dollars in traveler's checks, every penny she possessed, with her. She was a pauper!

Weakly she sank to a chair, which was where she was sitting when Clint reappeared. Seeing the pallor of shock on her face, he rushed over and knelt next to her.

"Sierra, what's wrong?"

"I—I'm broke. Completely broke."

"Are you talking about money? Do you think I give a damn if you don't have any?"

"I did have money, Clint. Quite a lot of money. It was in the van. Everything I owned was in the van."

He took her by her arms. "Sierra, it doesn't matter."

Her eyes looked dazed. "It does matter, Clint. Oh, I should have left it in the bank instead of buying all those traveler's checks." She was stunned when Clint started laughing. "Why are you laughing? It's not funny, Clint."

"Honey, if your money was in traveler's checks, you

can redeem them. Do you remember the name of the bank where you purchased the checks?''

''Yes.''

''Then all you have to do is contact the bank, explain what happened and they'll do the rest. You'll have your money, sweetheart.''

She suddenly felt silly for carrying on over something she should have remembered herself. Apparently her memory still wasn't a hundred percent.

But it was good enough! She threw her arms around Clint's neck. ''I'm not married,'' she whispered. ''Clint, I'm *not* married!''

''You're going to be,'' he said, just before he laid a passionate, loving kiss on her lips.

She kissed him back so enthusiastically that they were both breathing hard when they came up for air.

''Was that a marriage proposal I heard a minute ago?'' she whispered huskily.

''Damned right it was,'' he growled. Then he smiled lovingly. ''Not a good enough one, though.'' He was already on his knees, and he took her hand in his. ''Sierra Benning, beautiful, wonderful, sweet lady, will you marry me?''

''Oh, Clint, yes. Yes, yes, yes!''

Epilogue

With the blessing of regained memory, Sierra knew that she had never been happier in her life. Loving Clint, and having him love her in the same impassioned way, was like a miracle. She had left San Francisco looking for something—a life, a little happiness, *something*—and now she knew that what she'd really been looking for was love. The miracle was in actually finding it. Yes, she'd gone through hell for a while, but she would suffer it all again if it meant meeting Clint, and obviously it had. Without the accident they would not have met. No one would ever convince Sierra that fate hadn't led her up the Cougar Pass road.

She and Clint talked and talked. He wanted to know all about her past life, and it was so wonderful to know it herself that she was more than willing to describe people, places and events. He was especially interested in her family.

"I'm the middle child," Sierra explained. "My sister

Blythe is ten years older than I am, and my other sister, Tamara, is ten years younger.''

"You mean there are ten years between each of you? That's rather unusual.''

"It's *very* unusual, Clint.'' Her voice became quiet and a little sad. "I was nine when Blythe left home. She went to college, got married and moved to Connecticut. There was no chance of really getting to know her. Then, when Tamara was nine or ten, *I* left home. Almost the same story. College, job, marriage. Tamara and I were never close, either. Mostly we heard about each other from our mother. Last January, when she passed away…'' Sierra paused to think about that heartbreaking event and wiped away a tear before continuing. "We congregated in Coeur d'Alene for Mother's funeral, and it was the first time in years that the three of us were together. It felt…strange. We talked, of course, but not about anything close to our own hearts. I could have told them that my marriage was falling apart, for instance, but I never said a word about it.''

"Maybe you were just too unhappy to talk about it,'' Clint said quietly.

"No, that wasn't it. But normally we don't talk about our private lives to strangers, and that's what my sisters felt like to me—strangers.'' Sierra waved her hand. "Oh, not entirely, of course. We had the same mother and father, and there was that bond between us. But…'' She stopped to frown. "I don't fully grasp it, Clint. We're just not close, and other than our age differences, I don't know why.''

"You've called your sisters, haven't you?''

"Oh, yes. Corey Mason, too. They were all glad to hear from me. Relieved, too. You see, before I left San Francisco, I phoned Blythe and Tamara, told them about the divorce, finally, and that I was going to do some traveling. I couldn't tell them where I was going, because I didn't know myself. But they expected an occasional postcard or something to let them know I was still on the face of the earth. My complete silence worried them."

"Sierra, people don't worry about people they don't care about. I think there's a lot more closeness between you and your sisters than you've indicated."

Sierra drew a breath. "Well, there seems to be more than there used to be. It started at Mother's funeral. We spent a few days together in Mother's home."

"But you didn't talk about what each of you was doing with your life."

"Not really. It was…as though each of us was protecting or guarding a secret. I know I was." Her eyes narrowed thoughtfully. "And so was Tamara. She was pregnant. Ultimately she married the father, and I *think* they're happy, but who knows?" She paused, then added, "I pray they are."

"All of you were close to your mother, weren't you?"

"Well…in a way, yes. But there was something…" She stopped and shrugged. "I don't know what it was. Mother always maintained a certain reserve. She was a good and generous person with both her time and money. She was forever volunteering for some church event, and also for civic affairs. It's just that when I think of her…" Sierra became lost in thought for several moments, then went on. "I know she loved us, but she was not an emotional woman."

"Maybe she, too, had a secret." Clint wasn't serious. The idea of family members keeping secrets from each other seemed pretty far-fetched to him.

But Sierra took his comment very seriously. "I've wondered about that before, and I recall Tamara saying something to that effect, as well. It's possible."

"Okay, you had a secret, Tamara had one and you suspect your mother did. What about Blythe?"

"Blythe is harder to read. She's a quiet, gentle woman, highly intelligent. She put her teaching career in Connecticut on hold to see to Mother's estate, which is the reason she's living in Coeur d'Alene. She's a widow…oh, I already told you that. But she's been a widow for many years, and as attractive as she is—beautiful, really—one would think she would have remarried long ago."

Sierra's eyes narrowed slightly. "They're all blondes, you know. Blythe and Tamara took after Mother in that respect. I inherited Dad's dark hair and eyes. The vague image I saw of four blond women before my memory returned was Mother, Tamara, Blythe and my friend Corey."

Clint squeezed her hand and grinned. "I personally prefer brunettes."

"Glad you do," she said pertly. "You're sort of my ideal, too."

They basked in the wonder of their love for a minute, then started talking again.

"So," Clint said. "Blythe doesn't have a secret."

"I didn't say that. She has as much reserve as Mother did, only it's different, very hard to explain. Like I told you, we rarely saw each other, any of us, but whenever I was with Blythe I got this peculiar feeling, almost a sense of something huge and unspeakable." Sierra paused. "Actually, if I'm to be totally honest here, I think Blythe has the biggest secret of all."

Clint laughed. "Honey, *I* think you're letting your imagination get a little carried away with this 'secret' stuff."

Sierra smiled rather smugly. "You just might feel differently after you meet Tamara and Blythe. I promised each of them that we would visit."

"And when are we going to do that?" Clint asked teasingly.

"Well, a trip to Coeur d'Alene is a simple matter. It's not far from here. Going to Texas, of course, would take more time and planning. I explained to my sisters that we're having a simple wedding, just Rosie, Tommy, you, me and the preacher. But what about a traveling honeymoon? We could drive to Coeur d'Alene and see Blythe, then go on to Spokane and catch a plane for Dallas, rent a car and drive to Tamara and Sam's ranch. Clint, I want to show you off," she finished with a proud and perky smile.

"You do, huh? C'mere and let me show *you* a few things."

Laughing, she fell into his arms.

Clint wasn't the only person in the Barrow household Sierra talked to. She willingly satisfied Rosie's curiosity about her past and what was happening in the present with her and Clint, and Rosie was thrilled to death that a wedding was being planned, simple or otherwise.

Tommy was a different story. He was polite to Sierra, even friendly to a point, but he wasn't comfortable around her, which bothered her terribly. The thing was, she didn't feel that she should be the one to bring up the accident; Tommy should do that, and she wished so much that he would. She held nothing against him because of it, but how could she tell him when he so cautiously tiptoed around the subject?

On Wednesday morning she remembered her appointment with Dr. Trugood, scheduled for the following day, and she used the phone at Clint's desk to cancel it. It took only a few minutes to handle, and she was still sitting at the desk when the phone rang. Because she was right there next to it, she called out to Rosie, "I'll get it," then picked up the receiver and said, "Barrow Ranch."

"Sierra?"

"Officer Mann?"

"Hi, how're you doing?"

"If I was doing any better I'd be flying instead of walking. John, I have to thank you again. You're a tenacious investigator, thank God, and I for one appreciate your dedication to duty. Believe me, I will never forget what you did for me."

"Sierra, I only did my job."

"Well, you do your job better than anyone *I've* ever known." She laughed. "If you only knew how wonderful it is to be able to say something like that."

"I think I have a pretty good idea. Sierra, is Clint around?"

"He's out working, John. Would you like him to return your call when he comes in?"

"How about Tommy. Is he there?"

"He's with Clint, John, sorry. Can I take a message?"

"Yes, I think you can. It's not like I'd be telling you something you shouldn't know. I discussed Tommy's role in the accident with my captain, and he decided that since everything turned out so well, and Tommy's never been in any kind of trouble before, ticketing him would not be in anyone's best interest. If you'll pass that on to him—"

Thrilled and excited, Sierra cut in. "Oh, I will, I will, and I'm so glad your captain is an intelligent, understanding man."

"Well, it was Tommy's good record that swayed him, Sierra. A good kid deserves a second chance, in his book. Mine, too."

"I couldn't agree more. Thank you for calling, John. I'll tell Tommy the good news the minute I see him."

Sierra was on pins and needles waiting for Tommy to come in. The day dragged, and she just happened to be near a window at the exact moment he rode into the compound on horseback.

But he dismounted and headed into the barn, and she was afraid he wasn't going to come to the house. Clint must have sent him back for something, she thought, and she ran outside and down to the barn.

"Tommy?" she called as she walked in.

"I'm in the storage room, Sierra," he answered.

She hurried to the room where the supplies were stored.

He was loading a knapsack with the large, strong staples they used to repair barbed-wire fencing. His sleeves were rolled up, and there was sweat on his forehead and discoloring his shirt.

"Hot today," she said.

"Yeah, it is."

He wasn't quite looking at her, Sierra realized—not fully, not openly. He was ashamed and uncomfortable around her, and her heart went out to him.

"Tom, John Mann called and left a message for you."

Tommy turned slowly, wearing a downcast expression. "What'd he say?"

"They're not going to ticket you, mostly because of your exemplary record."

Tommy's eyes jerked up. "Really?"

Sierra smiled. "Really. Tommy, I'm very happy about their decision."

"You are? But—"

"No 'buts,' Tommy. I'd like to say something. Will you listen and believe me?"

He nodded, and Sierra could see that he was very close to tears, which would probably embarrass him completely if they fell. But this was the best opportunity she'd had to get through to Clint's son, and she had to take it.

"Tom, I hold no grudge about the accident. I want us to be friends. You know your father and I are going to be married, and I want the three of us to be a whole and happy family."

The tears that Sierra had feared were so close began seeping down Tommy's cheeks. He dropped the knapsack and wiped at them, leaving smears of dirt on his face.

"I couldn't see how you could ever like me," he said raggedly. "I'm so damned sorry, Sierra. I was so used to that road, and hardly anyone was ever on it. I was running behind that morning, and Eric and I were worried about getting to class late because of a test. It's no excuse for speeding on a dangerous road, I know, but…that's what happened.''

"Maybe you did wrong that morning, Tom, but which of us is perfect? I don't want this between us, Tommy. In fact, I never want to talk about it again. It's over, and guess what?'' She smiled. ''If it weren't for the accident, I would never have met your father.''

He blinked at her, and then he grinned. It was if the sun had suddenly come out. ''I never thought of it that way.''

"Well, do. I've never been happier, Tommy. I love the ranch, I love the area and I love…the two Barrow men.'' She hastened to add, ''Not that I will ever try to take your mother's place.''

Tommy was still grinning. ''Can…can I hug you?''

"Absolutely!'' She opened her arms.

In bed that night she told Clint all about it. ''And then he gave me a big bear hug. Oh, Clint, everything is perfect now.''

He raised up on an elbow to look into her eyes. ''Maybe it didn't seem so for a while there, but it's been perfect all along, sweetheart. Life started being perfect the second I set eyes on you.''

She lovingly touched his face. ''I love you so much.''

"I love you.'' He kissed her tenderly, adoringly, then lay back on his pillow.

As Clint fell asleep, she thought of all that had happened. So much uncertainty, so many emotionally chaotic days and nights.

But it was over now, just another segment of her past. What was most important was that she had been looking for love, and she'd found it.

Oh, yes, everything was perfect, she thought, and closed her eyes with a sigh of utter contentment. Tomorrow would be another glorious day. She was sure of it.

*   *   *   *   *

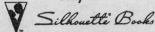

Take 2 bestselling love stories FREE

Plus get a FREE surprise gift!

Special Limited-Time Offer

Mail to Silhouette Reader Service™

P.O. Box 609
Fort Erie, Ontario
L2A 5X3

YES! Please send me 2 free Silhouette Desire® novels and my free surprise gift. Then send me 6 brand-new novels every month, which I will receive months before they appear in bookstores. Bill me at the low price of $3.49 each plus 25¢ delivery and GST*. That's the complete price, and a saving of over 10% off the cover prices—quite a bargain! I understand that accepting the books and gift places me under no obligation ever to buy any books. I can always return a shipment and cancel at any time. Even if I never buy another book from Silhouette, the 2 free books and the surprise gift are mine to keep forever.

326 SEN CH7V

Name	(PLEASE PRINT)	
Address		Apt. No.
City	Province	Postal Code

This offer is limited to one order per household and not valid to present Silhouette Desire® subscribers. *Terms and prices are subject to change without notice. Canadian residents will be charged applicable provincial taxes and GST.

CDES-98   ©1990 Harlequin Enterprises Limited

Available September 1998
from Silhouette Books...

World's Most
Eligible Bachelors

THE CATCH
OF CONARD COUNTY
by Rachel Lee

Rancher Jeff Cumberland: long, lean, sexy as sin. He's
eluded every marriage-minded female in the county.
Until a mysterious woman breezes into town and
brings her fierce passion to his bed. Will this steamy
Conard County courtship take September's hottest
bachelor off of the singles market?

Each month, Silhouette Books brings you
an irresistible bachelor in these all-new,
original stories. Find out how the sexiest,
most sought-after men are finally caught...

Available at your favorite retail outlet.

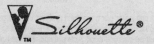

Silhouette®

MATERNITY LEAVE

Coming September 1998

Three delightful stories about the blessings
and surprises of "Labor" Day.

TABLOID BABY by Candace Camp

She was whisked to the hospital in the nick of time....

THE NINE-MONTH KNIGHT
by Cait London

A down-on-her-luck secretary is experiencing
odd little midnight cravings....

THE PATERNITY TEST by Sherryl Woods

The stick turned blue before her
biological clock struck twelve....

*These three special women are very pregnant...and very
single, although they won't be either for too much longer,
because baby—and Daddy—are on their way!*

Available at your favorite retail outlet.

SILHOUETTE® *Desire®*

COMING NEXT MONTH